THE BILLIONAIRE'S FORBIDDEN KISS

A BEST FRIEND'S FORBIDDEN OLDER BROTHER ROMANCE.

LEXI AURORA

1

JENNA

I knocked on my best friend Casey's door, waiting nervously for her to answer it. I hadn't seen Casey in a year and even then our visits had been short and sporadic since high school. It'd been hard for me to face her, knowing full well that I broke our pact all those years ago. Besides, I'd been busy at school.

The front porch looked just as I remembered it. Filled with flower arrangements and sleek outdoor furniture that accented the giant house beautifully. Casey still lived in her childhood home in Maplewood, New Jersey with her mom, Alice. Being here again was like being transported back to my own childhood. I used to spend days here at a time—entire weekends when my mom was at art shows. I remembered running in and out of this house, playing around the neighborhood with Casey and her brother, Travis.

Casey pushed her door open and her face lit up. She threw her arms around me, pulling me in for a tight hug. In that moment, I knew I made the right choice coming here. I needed this.

"Jenna! What are you doing here? And why are you

knocking?" she asked, tugging me by the arm into the house behind her. "You never knock."

"I haven't been here in a year," I said, laughing. "I didn't think I could just walk in."

"You never have to knock," she said, waving me off as I followed her through the front hallway and into her living room, where she had pizza and wine splayed on the coffee table. I stood at the base of the table, anxiously rubbing my hands together and staring at the ground.

"What's wrong, babes?" Casey asked, sensing my discomfort.

"I didn't know where else to go. It's my mom again. You know her," I responded, meeting her stare.

"Ugh, what happened? Is that why you're back in town?"

I told Casey everything. I told her how my mom called me, saying that she was finally going to take a short break from work and that she'd be back home for my spring break. She said she wanted to spend the week with me, so I left Yale for the break, excited to see her. But once I got home, I found a note on our kitchen counter. An art gallery in the city was hosting an auction this weekend and a spot had opened up for her. So she took it, saying it was a big opportunity to get her work seen by a new crowd, and I was left disappointed by my mother yet again. I'm not sure why I was surprised. I was always coming second to her art.

Casey grabbed my hand and squeezed it, an apologetic expression on her face. She had a way of making you feel special just by looking at you, and within minutes I found myself settling into a familiar feeling of comfort and love with my friend, as if we hadn't been apart for months. My worries about my mother slowly washed away.

"Well, I'm so glad you're here. Let's have a girls night to

cheer you up! My mom is also in the city, so it'll just be us!" Casey said.

"That sounds amazing."

"So how have you been otherwise?" she asked. "You look great—tired, but great."

"I am tired," I said, leaning back against the couch and sinking into it. "I'm in my final year of school. I have endless work to do, and I feel like I never sleep."

"I can't believe you keep going through school," my friend said. "And at an Ivy League. No wonder you have so much work to do."

"I think it'll be worth it, though," I told her. I had been sure at one point—when I first took on all the loans I'd needed to go to Yale and live on campus, I had felt like there was nothing stopping me. Now, as I'd progressed through school, I'd only grown more and more unsure about my future. I was studying journalism, in hopes I could have a career in writing, but I was growing less and less confident in that decision. "I hope it'll be worth it. With as much debt as I'm in—"

"You need to marry a rich man to take care of your loans," Casey said, looking up at the ceiling, her voice dreamy. "That's what I'm looking for."

I laughed, but didn't respond. The truth was, I'd only had my eye on one man my entire life and it was Casey's brother, Travis, who was completely off-limits. He was also ridiculously rich, but I had fallen for him far before he had made his fortune, back when we were kids and he had given me my first kiss at his graduation party.

Just then Casey's phone went off and she reached into her purse to pull it out. I glanced at the screen to see Travis' face, waiting patiently for her to pick up a video call. My heart fluttered in my chest, something like panic coursed through me as I quickly snuck my hands up to my face and pushed my hair back, smoothing the front of my shirt down. I hadn't seen Travis since that last night he kissed me, the night I had broken my pact, but I'd thought about him ever since.

It was my first and only kiss. His soft lips grazed mine and butterflies exploded in my stomach while time paused, infinite and fleeting all at once. Then he pulled away, shook his head, and told me that I was like a sister to him. He disappeared the next day, rushing off to LA to start his life outside of Maplewood.

Casey answered the call and the screen widened to show Travis, a grin on his handsome face. I kept myself out of view. I was nervous to talk to Travis, especially in front of Casey. Throughout school, Casey always got extremely annoyed whenever any girl mentioned that they thought her brother was hot. She had been glad to make friends with me knowing that I didn't have any interest in him, that I was her friend alone. On the day Casey and I met, she had sat down next to me in our middle school cafeteria during lunch period, not shy at all. She introduced herself and we basically didn't stop talking to each other for the next five years, until graduation.

Eventually I found out that she had sat by me that day because her previous best friend had asked her for Travis' phone number, and when she refused, the girl got angry. Casey realized that she had only been her friend to get to Travis, and this wasn't the last time it had happened. Travis was hot in high school, every girl fawned over him, and many of the girls thought Casey would be an easy ticket to get to him. At first, I didn't think about Travis in that way. But he and his family took care of me over the years, my dad having left when I was young, and my mom being such a flake. Soon, I couldn't stop thinking about Travis, but I didn't want to hurt Casey. I had kept my crush on him private for that reason, and wasn't sure that I would be able to hide my feelings for him if I had to talk to him for the first time right in front of her.

"What's up?" said Casey, her voice excited. She and her brother had always been close, and I knew that they had these video calls at least once a week while they were apart in separate cities.

"Hey, sis," Travis said, and just the sound of his voice made something shift in my body, made my stomach feel light and fluttery. He was so handsome—his dark hair was pushed back from his face, his hazel eyes sparkling with light. Casey caught me off-guard by turning the camera toward me then, and I watched Travis' face light up when he saw me. I opened my mouth to say hello, but I could only stare at him. I hoped to God that Casey didn't notice the pause between us as we drank each other in for a moment.

"Hi," I said to him finally, breaking the silence.

"Jenna," he said. "Wow."

"Um, I was just over here visiting Casey. How are you?"

"I'm good," he said, looking over at Casey, then back at me. "How are you guys?"

"We're good," I said, my throat dry. I had to look away from the screen. I felt his eyes on me as Casey started to speak. He was studying my face intently, making me blush under his gaze. I only hoped that Casey didn't notice my reaction; not only would it be embarrassing, but I was sure that she would be angry at me if she found out how I felt about her brother, that I had always carried a torch for him even when we were kids.

"So are you ready for this big family bash, Travis?" she asked. "It's going to be crazy."

"It is going to be interesting," he said, rubbing his hand over his mouth. His eyes were still on me even as he spoke to his sister, and I prayed that he would look away from me before she noticed how focused he was. I searched his face for any clue that he was remembering our kiss too.

"Why don't you come, Jenna?" Travis asked. I blinked at him, looking over at Casey. I had zoned out and wasn't sure what he was talking about anymore. I hadn't been focused on anything but the memory of Travis' lips on mine.

"Come where?"

"On vacation!" Casey said. "It's my mom's fiftieth birthday. She would love it if you were there."

"I don't know, I—"

"Come on," said Travis. "It's a private island in the Florida Keys. My friend and I bought up the property to rent out to vacationers. But this week, it's all ours. Beautiful place. You'll love it."

"You definitely need a getaway, girl," Casey said.

She was right. I was exhausted and in desperate need of an escape. My alternative to going on the trip was to either spend spring break in my empty house in Maplewood or on the empty Yale campus, sulking about my mom.

"I guess I could go," I said, realizing that neither of them were going to let me say no anyway. A vacation sounded great, even if it meant hiding my attraction to Travis.

"Good," said Travis, who was chewing on his lip as he looked at me. "Good girl. Case, make sure you bring suntan lotion this time, you know—"

"Okay, dad," Casey said, rolling her eyes.

"I'm just saying," he said with a grin. "I'd better go. I'll send you the final details later today. See you later."

"Bye, Travis," I said softly, and he winked at us before he hung up. I was still feeling fidgety and warm as I had been while he was on screen. I looked at Casey, studying her face to find out if she noticed how I had been affected by Travis on the phone. She didn't look like she had—she was smiling and bouncy, excited that I was going to go on the vacation with her. I was excited, too. It meant that our couple of days together was going to expand into the full week. It also meant that I would have to see Travis in person, which I imagined would be much more difficult than seeing him smiling on a phone screen.

2

———

TRAVIS

I sat back in my leather office chair, spinning in a slow circle as I put the phone to my lips and thought of Jenna. I hadn't seen her since the night before I headed to LA, having finally inherited my dad's small fortune on my 18th birthday. I was determined to start my own business and support my family.

I remembered vividly the kiss we shared before I left—it had been soft and sweet, perfect; I'd wanted it to go deeper, to taste her mouth, but she had been so young and delicate. I knew we couldn't go that far. I was overwhelmed with how strong my feelings were for her, validated even more by our kiss. Overcome with emotion, I pulled away. I tried to tell her I loved her, but I got scared. I ran away from the most beautiful girl I'd ever laid eyes on.

She wasn't a young girl anymore, though, and she hadn't looked remotely delicate to me on the screen. Her strawberry-blonde hair was full, thick, and curly around a heart-shaped face. Those green eyes had been focused on me more intently than my sister had probably realized, and I knew in an instant that she was thinking the same thing I was.

But there was something sad in her eyes too. I noticed that Jenna wasn't entirely focussed, that her thoughts were elsewhere. She tried to hide it on the call, but seeing her so distraught had taken over my rational brain. I wanted so badly to make her feel better. At that moment, inviting her on the trip seemed like the perfect solution. I could cheer her up and finally finish what we started all those years ago. Now the spell had broken and reality set in; having her along on the island would complicate so much.

I stood up and left my office, going next door to see my business partner. His door was open, and I went inside, shutting it behind me. My partner, Arthur Monroe, was also my best friend and, aside from my sister, my closest confidant. But this wasn't something that I could talk to my sister about—I could never let on that I had feelings for Jenna. Casey would be heartbroken. I knew she would feel betrayed by the both of us. I couldn't stand the thought of it being that way between Casey and I, not when she was one of the most important people in my life. She had sacrificed so much for our family, and she deserved the world. My mom was beside herself when my dad died, and then I left to try to help my family through a successful career. Casey stayed behind to take care of our mom. I had been trying so hard these past few years to help make Casey's dreams come true, to repay her for everything she had to give up.

"What's up?" Arthur asked, propping his feet up on the desk.

"I may have just done something really stupid," I said.

"Again?" He was grinning. I nodded; I had to give him that—I was prone to making impulsive decisions that didn't always lead to the best of consequences.

"Does it have anything to do with a girl?"

"Yep," I said. He shook his head. "Always. That's why I don't date women."

"Right. That's why."

He chuckled. "So what did you do? Who is she?"

"You know my sister Casey? It's her best friend. We've known each other since we were kids. I saw her on a video call with my sister and I invited her to our family vacation next week."

"Why'd you do that?"

"I want her," I said. "Seeing her again brought it all back. I had the biggest crush on her in high school and now she's even hotter."

"So what's the big deal?" he asked, folding his arms across his chest. "She married? Got a kid?"

"Casey would never go for it. She would hate both of us."

Arthur rolled his eyes. He had never been the type of person to care how other people felt about his decisions, which was why I had chosen him as my partner. He was a ruthless businessman, intent on getting what he wanted, and was the only person I'd met who matched me in terms of ambition and drive.

"She would get over it."

"I can't take the risk," I said. "I just—the moment I saw her again, I knew I had to have her. I have to."

"So do it," Arthur shrugged. "Keep it a secret while you're there. It'll make for some killer sex."

I knew that was true. I could only imagine Jenna's mature body, since I left when she was still a sophomore. But I was sure it had filled out as she'd grown. Her face surely had. I wanted to touch her no matter how she had grown up—my main desire was to see that look in her eyes again, wide and caught off-guard. I knew I'd surprise her if I showed her all the things I could do to her body. But it didn't feel like it was just about the sex; I wanted to talk to Jenna again. She had always been so funny and sweet. It was agonizing being around her as a teenager and knowing I had to keep a respective distance.

"Is she coming with your sister to the island? How are you going to make it work?"

"I have a private jet and property on the island with plenty of room, so it's not like we're going to have to squeeze her in."

"That's kind of too bad. It'd be nice if you had to share a room."

I laughed. "Probably won't happen."

"I think you should go for it. At least have some kind of fling. Feels good to get someone you've wanted for a long time."

"I think I will," I said. I had been scared back in high school, overwhelmed by my feelings for her. And my ambitions to support my family were pulling me in a different direction. But I wasn't a teenager anymore—I had become a billionaire, built my business from the ground-up because I was capable and determined. I took what I wanted. And I wanted Jenna.

"I have to get back to work," he said. "Let me know how it goes."

"I will," I told him. "Wish me luck."

He gave me a thumbs-up and I stood up, leaving his office and going back into my own. I sat down and my phone vibrated on my desk in front of me, a text from my ex-girlfriend, Devinia.

Hey baby. Missing you. Come see me this week? (;

I rolled my eyes. I broke up with Devinia several months ago when I realized that she was just using me for my status.

She was gorgeous, blonde, and fit, but unable to make her big break in the model world yet. Devinia introduced herself to me at a bar in Beverly Hills, recognizing me from a recent cover shoot. I thought she was attractive, but we never connected much beyond that. Now our relationship was strictly professional. Her father was backing my next investment, so I had to put up with her, to keep things friendly until the deal was over.

Can't. Gone for the week. Celebrating my mom's 50th. I'll tty when I'm back.

I responded and put my phone down, my thoughts instantly back on Jenna. I felt good now, determined I was going to make up for lost time with Jenna. It wasn't just about the kiss or her body, but the fact that things had felt so pure between us before. If I were to make my move, I'd have to keep it on the down low, at least for now. I knew I had a ridiculous reputation as a playboy—women often threw themselves at me, but I didn't return the affection as often as the press would like people to believe. Still, if Devinia's dad caught wind of this fling, he might pull his investment. He once told me he didn't want to ruin his reputation by being associated with "my habits". My private island would be the perfect place to pursue something with Jenna quietly until the deal went through. I didn't know how it was going to go over with Casey, but I tried not to think about it. I had something special planned for her too, something that would lessen the blow after I made Jenna mine.

3

JENNA

"I really can't allow you guys to do this," I said to Casey and her mother, Alice, as we waited on the tarmac for the private jet to arrive. Alice was one of my favorite people—she was a character, with long, greying hair in a braid, loose clothes, and a house full of plants that I remember her talking to every morning as she watered them. She was like a second mom to me, taking care of me when mine wasn't around. After Casey's dad died when we were in middle school, Alice was devastated and her spunky personality softened a bit. I hadn't seen Alice in so long and I hoped that she had found some of that spunk again, with her daughter staying home from college to support her and her son finding such success.

"Travis is paying for everything," Alice insisted. "We told you that. He has no problem with paying for you, sweetheart."

"But—"

"No arguing. It's my birthday and I demand you be there. Besides, if you want to pay your way, you'd have to take it up with Travis. And there's no way he's going to let you pay him back."

I sighed. I felt guilty about the thought of going on this expensive trip for free, especially considering all Casey's family had done for me throughout my life. There had been many nights spent at Casey's house for dinner—sometimes those nights turned into long weekends with my dad gone and my mom's art pulling her in every direction except mine.

Casey reached over to pat my hand, then wrapped her arm around my shoulders and hugged me to her.

"You're family," she said. "You're like a sister to Travis. And you deserve this, Jen. Let us cheer you up a bit!"

I swallowed hard, a lump in my throat. Of course, that's all I was to Travis. We had shared one parting kiss, one that hadn't even allowed me to taste him fully. It had been nothing. I felt embarrassed for lingering on Travis as if there was something between us, but there had been a certain look in his eye on the phone that made me wonder—

"Besides," Casey continued, a playful smile on her face, "I'll bet Travis spoils his model girlfriends all the time. He can spoil us a bit too!"

Alice and Casey laughed at this. I forced my mouth into a smile, trying to find humor in the joke. The truth was, I hadn't really considered how much Travis could have changed since moving to LA. I tried to keep him from my thoughts, and I vowed never to stalk him on social media, knowing it would just make all of my unresolved feelings come rushing back. My stomach churned at the thought of him becoming such a player, dating beautiful models and rich socialites. He could have any girl he wanted. Why would he choose his sister's best friend from the hometown he fled?

"So, Casey," I began, hoping to change the subject, "How's the coffee shop?"

Casey's face lit up. "It's so great! I mean, hard work and mediocre pay, but I'm hoping my commitment will pay off in the long run."

"How so?" I asked.

"Well, the owner is getting old, and grumbles about needing to sell someday soon. And I've been saving up to buy the shop! I'd call it Casey's Cafe!" Her face grew even more animated as she said it. "I was even thinking I could keep it open later, and turn it into a swanky night spot for Maplewood."

"Wow, Case. That sounds amazing!"

"Thank you! I just think it would feel good to have something that's mine, you know? I mean we've seen how successful Travis has made his business. I want to do that for myself. To turn that coffee shop into a local attraction!"

"If anyone can do it, it's you," I told her and I meant it. Casey had a real go-getter attitude. I saw it in the way she cared for her mom and took her responsibilities on the chin. She deserved this dream.

It was then that I saw the jet fly in, beginning its descent. We backed up on the tarmac, going inside to shield ourselves from the wind as the jet landed in front of us. It was sleek and small, nothing like the giant airliners I was accustomed to. I looked at it in wonder as the staircase descended and Casey started to climb it. I followed her and almost gaped at what I saw. Inside, the jet was absolute luxury. There were several comfortable-looking chairs in the middle. Each one had a small table next to it that had already been arranged with individual plates of fresh fruits and what looked like mimosas. Casey grinned at me when she saw my face.

"Travis likes to show off," she said as she made her way to the center of the plane and took a seat in one of the chairs. I sat down, immediately relaxing into the cushions. I picked up the mimosa and sipped at it, immediately feeling the bubbles of the champagne in my stomach. I couldn't help but to start to feel excited for the trip.

"I think this is exactly what I need," I told Casey. I felt my troubles melting away already. I knew that I would feel energized by the beach and this vacation, something that I desperately needed to get through the rest of the semester, and whatever the hell would happen after it, with my sanity intact.

"I think we all need this," said Alice. "I'm so glad you decided to come with us."

I smiled at her, eating some of the fruit and drinking the never-ending mimosas throughout the flight. I was slightly tipsy by the time we got to the island, which appeared breathtaking even from the air. I looked down to see the blue of the ocean, the white sands on the beach, and the colorful old houses that dotted the island. There weren't very many—I could tell that it was an exclusive place, beautiful and quiet, even before we landed.

We made our way through the airport and outside. An immediate warmth hugged my body as I felt the moisture in the air touch my skin—it was sunny and hot, but not unbearably so. There was a car waiting for us outside, a stretch limo that comfortably sat us all, with even more champagne cooling in a bucket in the center. I decided to wait a little bit before drinking anymore—I was already excited enough as we drove through the streets of the small island.

It took us a while to get to the house, which awed me almost as much as the interior of the jet had. It was massive and modern, all sharp angles and glass. It was on the beach, too, one side of the house leading right up to the water. We went inside, which was even more beautiful. I had never seen anything as opulent and luxurious as the things I already experienced on this trip.

"So we're going straight to the beach, right?" Casey asked as we went upstairs to our rooms. "I'm going to change right now."

"Absolutely," I said, hurrying into my room and changing into my bikini, one that I may or may not have bought to look especially good on this trip, knowing Travis would be here. We grabbed our bags and made our way out to the beach, where there were tables and lounging chairs set up under umbrellas, as well as several to lie in and sunbathe. The water was gorgeous, crystal clear and blue as we sat down in our chairs. After a few moments, a waiter came up to us dressed in a suit. He was carrying a tray of sandwiches along with fruit and salads that he placed on the table for us as he pulled out a bottle of wine.

We drank and ate in the shade, warm and perfect. Then we spread lotion on our bodies and laid in the sun. Casey looked over to me and smiled, holding out her hand. I grabbed it and squeezed, feeling so grateful for her friendship and this experience.

Once a calmness had settled over us, I pulled out my journal to write. I recorded my thoughts every day, using writing as a sweet escape from reality. As I journaled about my lavish surroundings, a ping of jealousy coursed through my pen before I was able to stop it. Travis and his family deserved a place like this, and with how hard he worked to make his business a success after his inheritance, he definitely earned it. But as I looked at his beautiful mansion and out into the captivating ocean, I couldn't help but feel irrationally jealous. I've had to work my ass off at menial service jobs while in school and I'm still in so much debt. On top of all this, I'm pursuing a career that might not be feasible. I love journalism, but I don't know if I can pursue it if it won't pay the bills. I could only dream of such success as this. It was after only a few moments trying to shoo away these thoughts that I fell asleep, dozing off in the sunlight and comfort of the lounger.

I didn't know how much time passed before something woke me, the soft touch of a hand on my shoulder. I opened my eyes to see Travis in front of me, his hazel eyes soft on mine. I scrambled out of the chair, startled by seeing him. I stood up and quickly fell back down after bumping my head on an umbrella that I didn't remember being there when I dozed off. Casey must have covered me before going inside.

"Travis," I said from the ground, sinking into the warm sand and trying to recover from my embarrassing display. I stumbled over my words, mixing them up in my grogginess. "Where—how did you come from?"

He gave a soft laugh. My heart did a flip in my chest at the look on his face, the look in his eyes as they held mine. He reached his hand out to help me up and I took it, feeling the heat of his soft skin. It made a shiver run up and down my body that felt almost electric as his hand lingered on mine. We were standing close, neither one of us speaking, and I found myself looking at his lips, the memory of our kiss vivid in my mind. He was staring at me with the same look on his face that I'd imagined I must have had when I'd first seen his house—something like wonder and interest, something that made me feel light and airy.

"Hey, guys," said Casey, calling from a distance as she made her way toward us. I jumped away from Travis, tearing my eyes away from his. I knew that we had been standing much too close for comfort. It would have been obvious to Casey that Travis and I were drawn to each other, and it would do more than ruin the whole weekend—it could ruin my friendship with her.

We started to head inside as Casey came into view and waved us in. As we walked, Travis bumped up against me on purpose, giving me a sly smile when I looked up at him. It felt as if no time had passed, although I saw something in his eyes—a hint of mischief that told me he was very well aware of how much time had passed and how much I'd changed. I hadn't missed the fact that he'd taken a few seconds to look me over in my bikini when he'd first seen me. Maybe he was interested in me after all, which meant that I was in for a lot of trouble on this trip.

4

———

TRAVIS

Seeing Jenna again had affected me even more deeply than I had thought it would when I first invited her. Something had swirled in my chest, a tight feeling when I saw her sleeping, peaceful face. Her lashes were spread across her cheeks, her full lips opened slightly. She was wearing a red bikini, one that made it almost impossible not to look over every inch of her body. I stopped at her stomach, noticing her splayed journal, and I smiled at the sight. She had been such a good writer in high school, so passionate about it. I was glad she was still pursuing it. I would have continued to take in her beautiful features, but it felt wrong to gaze at her body without her knowledge.

I had woken her up after a few moments of watching her sleep, and had not expected her startled reaction. I'd noticed the way she reacted when I touched her though, and had been able to sense the fact that she'd wanted that skin contact as much as I did. She had been so close to me, her body almost touching mine, and if Casey hadn't interrupted I had no doubt that I would have ended up touching

Jenna again. The impulse had been almost too strong to resist after the first touch.

I was pretty sure that Jenna was interested in me but I wanted to keep testing it, to find out subtly rather than just coming out and asking her or making too many assumptions. When I took Jenna, I wanted her to be all in, to give herself to me with no inhibitions. I had to be sure before I made a move; I couldn't do it if she was uncomfortable with me. There was no way I could take the thought of making Jenna feel uncomfortable when all I wanted to do was pull her against my body.

We went inside the house, walking across the beach together. I wanted to take her hand but I didn't, knowing that Casey was watching us as we made our way back to the house. Inside, my mom was waiting in the living room. When she saw me, she stood up, opening her arms wide. I hugged her, grateful to see her. I had always been close with my family, especially after my dad passed. I was more than glad to see them in person after so many Skype calls.

Once I'd greeted my mom and Casey, I couldn't keep my eyes off Jenna as we all sat down in the living room to have drinks before dinner. She was sipping a glass of wine, her eyes occasionally meeting mine.

"What have you been up to, Jenna?" I asked her. I wanted to know everything about her, every detail of her life.

"I'm in my last semester at Yale," she said. "Just finishing up. Crazy busy. I don't even think I should be taking this time off."

"You deserve to take time off," I said to her. "I think you need to relax."

She licked her lips. "You're probably right."

"I am right," I said.

"What are you studying?" I asked her. I wished my mom wasn't there, that Casey wasn't there. I wanted to talk to Jenna alone and hoped that I would get the opportunity to do so soon.

"Journalism," she said.

"I'm sure you're amazing at it." I'd known that Jenna was smart in high school, but I hadn't known how smart. She had been a few grades below me and I had only paid attention to her through the lens of my crush—I had known that she was beautiful and sweet and that had been enough for me as a teenager. Now, I knew better, and the fact that Jenna was working so hard was a massive turn-on.

"That is so impressive," Alice said, waving her fork at Jenna. "I could never do that. How much does it cost to go to a school like Yale?"

I shot a look at my mother, but she was intent on Jenna, apparently unaware of how rude her question was to ask.

"It's a lot," Jenna admitted. "Luckily, I got it all covered with loans."

"You took out loans?" I asked. I hated the idea of that. There was no reason that anyone I cared for should ever have to be in debt, not with as much money as I made.

"I had a few scholarships, but it's been loans for the most part."

"I can pay—"

"I'm going to pay you back for this trip," she interrupted me. "I just need you to tell me how much my portion is going to cost."

"No."

"Travis—"

"You're family, Jen," I said. "You belong here."

"Oh," she said, biting her lip. She looked away from me then, turning her eyes to Casey. I could tell that she was hoping somebody would change the subject; it seemed like the money situation embarrassed her, and I could understand why. My family hadn't always been rich.

"Thank you," she said after a moment. She took another drink of her wine, her foot bouncing nervously as we waited for dinner. I tried to catch her eye but I couldn't—she was looking decidedly away from me. I wondered if it was the money thing or if it was something else. I only knew I wanted to fix it, to see the look of interest in her pretty green eyes again.

"I'm going to run up to my room for a minute and change," she said, standing up abruptly. "It's hot in here."

"Okay," my mom said.

I watched as Jenna disappeared up the stairs. She glanced at me over her shoulder when she got up there, giving me a look that was unreadable. I had no idea what to expect from Jenna on this trip, but I had a feeling that it was going to drive me absolutely crazy.

5

JENNA

I sat down on my bed for a moment, looking at my hands. I remembered Travis' words clearly—I was family to him, something like a sister. I was just his little sister's friend. I felt embarrassed that I had thought there was something between us. Based on what Casey had said on the plane, he could have any model he wanted. I was relieved, though, that the trip would no longer be complicated by the temptation of kissing Travis again.

Casey came into the room then, a small frown on her face as she looked at mine. She had always been able to read me even since we were kids. Not only was she astute on her own, but she knew me like the back of her hand by now. In this case, I regretted that aspect of our closeness. It meant that it was hard to hide anything from her.

"What's wrong?"

"Nothing," I said quickly, making sure that I didn't avoid her eye. I had no doubt that she would know I was lying if I showed it in any way, so I kept my expression carefully blank.

"Okay. Well you know you can tell me if something is.

Anything," she said, sitting on the bed next to me. She was looking at my face, studying it for any sign that I wasn't okay. I smiled at her and nodded. After a minute, I got up and changed, then we went downstairs for dinner when we heard Alice calling us from the back patio. Casey sat next to her brother and I sat across from him, trying not to meet his eye over the table. I could feel his gaze on my skin like a caress, a subtle warmth. It confused me—Travis had called me family but at the same time I would have sworn that he was attracted to me. In any other situation, that look would be unmistakable.

Instead of looking at him, I looked out at the ocean, the waves crashing against the rocks a few miles from our beach. The sun was going down over the water, and for a moment it felt like the most beautiful thing I had ever seen.

"What do you think?" Travis asked. I turned around to look at him and made the mistake of meeting his eyes. He held me captivated there, unable to look away.

"I think it's perfect here," I told him.

"Did you ever think you would own a house like this, Travis?" Casey asked. I could see some jealousy in her face, remembering her dream to own the coffee shop.

"No," said Travis. "I had no idea my company would blow up so big. I thought I was going to go to college when I was a teenager."

"I thought I wasn't," I said.

"And look at you now. I've got no degree and you're at Yale."

"You're a billionaire, sweetie," Alice said to her son. "I think you're doing okay. You've accomplished more than enough without a degree."

"I think he's spoiled," said Casey, mischievously grinning at her brother. "Don't you, Jen?"

I didn't look at her, couldn't look away from Travis. "I think he's something," I said. "Spoiled might be it."

He laughed, raising his eyebrows at me. "Oh?"

I nodded.

"If that's what I am, I don't mind it. I would never go back to the way things were before, when we were kids."

I squirmed uncomfortably, surprised by how much the words stung me. Earlier, standing with Travis, I would have given anything to go back in time and relive that kiss with him over and over. I wanted to go back to the days when I'd catch a glimpse of him while I was hanging out with Casey. I remembered that each time my heart had fluttered, and I'd wound up giggly, having to explain myself to Casey.

"Why not?" I asked him.

"I'm happier now," he said. "I have all I want. I'll never have to worry about money again."

"Money's not everything," I told him.

"She's right," said Alice, wrapping her arm around Casey's shoulder and hugging her affectionately. "Love is good." I could see the gratitude in Alice's eyes, at Casey for taking care of her all these years, and at Travis' determination to support them both. I could also see a hint of sadness, feeling the loss of her husband in this moment.

"I'm not looking for love right now," Travis said, but he had glanced at me when she first said it. I was sure that I was reading too much into things, but that didn't stop my chest from feeling full.

"I am," said Casey. "Do you have any billionaire friends?"

"A couple. But you wouldn't like them."

"Why not?" she asked.

"Because they're fat, old, and bald."

She wrinkled up her face. "Gross. Although, maybe

they'd treat me better than the jerks I've dated that were my age."

"Yeah, maybe," he said, laughing. I was feeling full already, the fresh fish we were eating was so good that I had kept going just to taste it. Once everybody was finished eating dinner, we went back into the living room. I sank into the couch cushions, feeling full and sleepy again, as if I hadn't taken a nap that afternoon. My eyelids were low but I was enjoying the conversation, the warmth of the family and the comfort of being in the beautiful house.

Dessert was served to us by two waiters, who brought out small plates of cakes and even more champagne. For a moment, it made me feel out of place, all the decadence, like I didn't belong here. I looked at Travis and I could see how content he was. He had changed so much in order to achieve all this, and he said he'd never go back. He didn't miss high school and I couldn't blame him. I mean, look at where he'd gotten. I just wished that I could shake my lingering feelings for the past as easily as he seemed to.

6

———

TRAVIS

"I think I'm going to bed," my mom said, standing up and stretching. I looked over to see that Casey had already passed out on the couch. I hadn't been paying attention to anything other than Jenna, sneaking glimpses at her sleepy face, the relaxed smile, the lean posture of her body melting into the couch. I was privately hoping that Jenna wouldn't get up to join them, and when she stayed put I felt relieved. I looked over at her and she finally looked back.

"Would you like to go for a walk with me?" I asked.. She seemed to have to think about it, because it took her a moment to answer. She nodded at me and we made our way to the beach, kicking off our shoes so that we could walk barefoot in the sand. It still felt warm on my feet, even though it was dark outside, and the air around us felt the same. The water was cool, though, lapping at our feet as we walked side-by-side along the beach in silence. I didn't end up taking in much of the scenery—my focus was on Jenna, even when I wasn't looking at her. I was thinking of the right thing to say, wondering how to start a conversation without blurting out my feelings for her against my will.

"How is your life in Los Angeles?" she asked finally, looking over at my face while we walked.

"It's good. Life is very good. I work a lot, but I'm happy."

"What exactly do you do as a property developer?"

"My partner and I finance properties. Basically, we reimagine their use, buy them up, and turn them into a more successful business."

"That is amazing," she said. "I can't imagine doing anything that big. How can you manage all that?"

"You will," I said to her. I wanted desperately to take her hand while we walked but instead I just let the backs of my fingers brush against her knuckles. I thought that she would pull away, but instead she traced my palm with the tips of her fingers, not quite holding my hand but making sure to touch it. It was a game as we walked, one that was building the lust in me higher and higher. It was almost uncontrollable.

"It takes a lot to keep it afloat. We have to find outside investors and maintain relationships with them, hold up our end of the bargains. It can be...difficult," I told her, thinking about my deal with Devinia's father.

"Do you—do you have a girlfriend in Los Angeles?" she asked, her voice shy.

"No," I told her. "No, I don't. I mean, I did, but we broke up."

"Oh," was all she said.

"It was never much of a relationship in the first place. Her name was Devinia. She was a model looking to work her way up the industry ladder by dating me," I tried to reassure her. Jenna laughed a little at this.

"What is it?" I asked.

"Nothing. It's just, on the plane Casey was going off about all of your model girlfriends and how you spoil them. She made you out to be quite the charmer," she responded, still giggling a bit.

There was silence for a moment before I opened my mouth to speak. I tugged at the neck of my shirt, growing a little hot at the mention of my status as a player.

"Don't believe everything you hear about my reputation."

Jenna was a little startled by the sudden seriousness. I cursed myself for ruining the moment. I decided now was a good time to be as open as possible. After all, I wanted Jenna to know me as much as I needed to know her.

"Casey was right about one thing though," I continued, trying to lighten the conversation back up. "I do like to spoil the women in my life." I smirked at Jenna and watched as she blushed.

The words came rolling out before I could stop them, fueled by the desire to touch her.

"Jenna," I said, taking her wrist, stopping her from walking. We stood there on the beach and I looked her in the eyes as I spoke. "I—you—it's good to see you."

She smiled, looking flattered by the compliment. "It's good to see you too."

"I never imagined what you would be like all grown up."

"You didn't?" she asked, a playful gleam in her eye.

"I knew you were beautiful," I said. "I knew you were—something better than perfect. I didn't think it was possible for you to get any more perfect."

She only stared at me for a moment, the smile no longer on her face. She bit her bottom lip.

"Do you remember the first time I kissed you?" I asked her in a soft voice, stepping close to her in the sand. I touched her face, stroking her jaw with my finger. I could feel her trembling, almost but not quite touching me.

"Yes," she said. "The first and only time."

I leaned in to brush my lips over hers.

"Not the only time," I said, kissing her softly, taking her bottom lip between mine and sucking on it. She pulled away from me before I could kiss her fully, a hesitant look on her face.

"Casey—"

"Forget about Casey," I said, though I knew I would feel guilty about it later. Right now, I wasn't thinking about my sister. I was thinking about Jenna and how badly I wanted her, more than I had ever wanted anything. She shook her head and stepped back, but she did allow me to take her hand, linking our fingers as we walked back to the house. Everything inside of me wanted to pick her up and carry her over the threshold, take her to my bedroom and fuck her nice and slow. But she was reluctant, which meant that I had to wait for her to make the first move. I didn't want this to be like my previous relationships. I couldn't rush it. We were still walking the beach, back towards the house when I got the one phone call from work I couldn't ignore.

7

JENNA

Travis's phone buzzed in his pocket and he let go of my hand to grab it.

"Damn." He looked up at me. "It's work. I have to take it." He apologized and walked a few paces ahead of me to take the call. I felt a twinge of panic in my stomach, his sudden departure bringing back the same sour feeling that my mom would give me whenever she'd leave me for her work. I could never be in another relationship like that again, one where work came before me. But the feeling fell away quickly.

I was still reeling from the kiss, my lips tingling from his touch. My stomach was doing flips as I replayed the moment in my head, over and over again. Then I thought about Casey and the flips in my stomach continued for an entirely different reason. I knew this would hurt her if I let it go any farther. She had lost several friends to her brother, and while I knew I would never treat her the way they did, no matter my relationship with Travis, I was sure she'd feel betrayed nonetheless.

Casey's broken friendships had left her unable to trust

most people. When they weren't using her to get to Travis, they were often pitying her for the loss of her father. She trusted me though—I made a pact to never pity her and never date her brother—and I didn't want to lose that trust, even for a moment. In time, she might forgive me, but I wasn't sure if our friendship would be the same if she knew I broke that pact.

In the distance, Travis grew animated. I could hear him muttering obscenities and I watched as he rubbed his stubbled jawline in agitated movements. I grew distracted, fixating on his chiseled features until the topic of his conversation stopped me in my tracks.

I could only make out bits and pieces, the roar of the waves overpowering his words. "Devinia will just have to wait...photoshoot...the deal can't fall...fine."

My thoughts began swirling the moment her name came out of his mouth. I had already made up my mind that it would be wrong to take things any further with Travis after that long-awaited, tender kiss. But now I was grappling with new feelings of confusion. Was Travis lying to me about his relationship status with Devinia? Did it even matter? I couldn't be with him anyway, but I couldn't help myself. I pulled my phone out and opened Google. I looked up the names Travis Winn and Devinia.

Several photos of Travis and Devinia together popped up and I clicked on one, the link redirecting me to Devinia's Instagram profile. I scrolled through her feed. She was just as beautiful as I'd imagined she'd be, if not more. Her hair was long and blond, and her tan body was slender. Her feed consisted mostly of lingerie and bikini shots, but I stopped scrolling once I reached the photo I had come here for, the one of her and Travis. He was looking directly into the camera, his hazel eyes focused and narrow. He was shirtless, wearing only a pair of boxer briefs. Devinia was wearing a black lacey bra and panties, her hair primped and her makeup flawless. Her gaze was on Travis, and I could see desire in her stare. I kept scrolling, my stomach in knots. There were only a few more photos of her and Travis, her feed mostly just of her. Most were clearly from photo shoots, but one was a selfie. Travis was looking off into the distance as Devinia made a kissy face at the camera. The caption read, "Quick coffee with Travy before a biz meeting. Working up something stunning! #WorkingGirl."

My scrolling was interrupted when Travis hung up the phone and made his way back to my frozen stance in the sand. He apologized again for the interruption and I hoped he'd asked *"where were we?"* or something equally cheesy, but the magic has passed; we walked back to the house in silence. Travis tried to get more conversation out of me, but I had nothing left to say. I was still processing everything that had happened on this walk.

We made it back and I laid down in bed, my mind focused on Travis. I had gone from complete elation to devastation in a matter of minutes. I was mad at myself for being so flustered at the mention of Devinia's name, especially after already deciding we couldn't be together. Then I realized what I was feeling deep in my chest: jealousy. I was jealous of Devinia, how easy it probably was for her to catch Travis' attention. How drop-dead gorgeous she was, and how perfect she looked standing next to Travis in that photo.

I stopped those thoughts before they could go any further. No, I wasn't a stunningly beautiful and insanely fit model like Devinia, but Travis kissed me on that beach, and I saw the way he looked at me, his eyes filled with something like desire. Something about me pulled him in. I knew

I could make him feel better than Devinia ever did, and I imagined what would have happened if I'd let him kiss me again on the beach. I regretted stopping him now—I had regretted it the moment I said no. I had to forcefully remind myself of Casey and the way she would feel about me kissing her brother. No matter how hard I tried, though, I couldn't help but think about kissing Travis, and then going even further. My pussy had never been so wet, swollen, and sensitive as it had been when he was standing close to me. I had almost been breathless with my desire for him. I still was.

I rolled over in bed, trying to get comfortable. I couldn't ease the ache between my legs no matter how hard I tried. I stroked myself but to no avail; I needed Travis' hands on me instead. I got up then, my body almost moving automatically as I slipped out of my bedroom and down the hall to Travis'. I didn't knock on the door. Instead I quietly tip-toed into the room, locking it behind me. Travis was in his bed, awake in the dark. His eyes met mine immediately, and his lips parted to speak.

"Jenna—"

"I heard some of your phone call on the beach. I need you to tell me that things are over between you and Devinia, and mean it," I told him, serious but seductive as I continued to imagine his touch. There was a shocked silence that made me nervous.

I desperately tried to overcome my nerves, shaking my head and twirling my hair as I waited for him to respond. I had never been this bold before, and I'd never even come close to another man's bed. My stomach was a ball of fire.

"I promise you things are over with her. They have been for a long time. That call was purely business, as is everything with Devinia now," he told me, his eyes holding mine to prove his words were true. He motioned for me to come closer and this gave me the confidence boost I needed.

His expression grew surprised as I reached down to my thighs and pulled off the thin nightgown I was wearing, baring myself to him. I wasn't wearing any panties and I felt like he could see how wet I was even in the dark, something that made me blush despite my boldness. He pulled back the covers to show that he was naked, gesturing for me to climb on top of him. Instead, I stood beside his bed, leaning over to take his lips in a soft kiss.

"Do you think of me as your sister, Travis?" I asked him, beyond control of my words. He shook his head, looking at my lips before he lifted his face to kiss me back.

"How do you think of me then?"

"Obsessively," he said. "I think about how you would taste—not just your mouth, but your pussy and your skin. I think about what it would be like to watch your face while you're wrapped around my cock."

I kissed him again, slipping my tongue into his mouth. His words put a fervor in me that I had never felt before, but I was waiting, keeping myself on edge, not quite ready to take the last step of climbing into bed with him.

"What else?" I asked him, my lips against his.

"I think about how sweet you are in other ways," he said in a voice that was low, almost a whisper. "Such a good, sweet girl."

I climbed on top of him then, straddling his hips so that my pussy was pressed against the length of his cock. When I grinded my hips forward, I could feel the head of it rubbing my clit. I started to move back and forth on him slowly, only teasing both of us. Something was making me hesitate, though my desire was overwhelming. Underneath me, Travis' hands were on my hips, tracing the curve of my waist before cupping my breasts in his hands. He teased the nipples with his fingertips, which grew even harder under his touch.

"Are you going to be a good girl for me and take my cock, Jenna? You gonna let me find out how sweet you are?"

I kissed him and nodded again, wanting nothing more than that. When he talked like that, my body felt like it had no choice but to give in.

He reached over into his side table and pulled out a small foil package, ripping it open. I lifted my hips up so that he could roll it down over his cock, then aimed himself inside of me and put his hands on my hips to lower me down, moving me slowly, filling me up with a deliberate stroke that took my breath away. I felt my pussy stretch to accommodate him, felt him hitting the back of my walls as deep as he could go. My body started rocking against his before I even planned my movements, finding a rhythm that made my toes curl and riding it again and again. Below me he kissed my neck, sinking his teeth into it as he started to lift his hips to meet with mine. Each stroke of his hips from below sent a wave of pleasure crashing into my body.

"God, you are so fucking perfect," he breathed, speaking into my ear as his hands found my ass and started to bounce my hips against him. I moaned in response and sat up so that I could look down at his face. I wanted to see him as I obeyed the command he was giving with his hands, to bounce against him, each thrust so deep it left me, once again, breathless.

He sat up then, pressing our chest together so that we were sitting up and face-to-face. He kissed me deeply, riding up against me, our bodies moving naturally together as if they were supposed to be that way.

"Travis," I moaned as I rocked against him. "You are so good."

He grinned, nipping on my lip before lowering his face to kiss the tops of my breasts. I arched back to give him access to my nipples, and he wrapped his lips around one of them and sucked on it gently. Too gently. His tongue teased instead of pleasured, and I desperately needed more from him. I ran my hands through his hair and sped my hips up, hoping that he would get the message that I could take things a little harder than he was giving them to me. He responded by teasing the other nipple instead, making me whimper with need.

"Goddammit," I moaned. "I hate being teased."

"And yet you're about to come all over me," he said, and I knew it was true. I was bucking forward against him, out of control of my hips. He tightened his lips around my nipple then and truly sucked on it, circling it with his tongue. He did the same to the other breast as he lifted his hips against mine. He lifted his face again to look at me, tracing my lips with his fingers before kissing me. The taste of his tongue combined with his hip movements, the feeling of his hands making me move faster, was enough to send me over the edge. I started to come hard, crying out before Travis put his hand over my mouth to stifle the rest of my moan.

He continued to fuck me then, only his movements were erratic, responding to each motion of my own body with a rhythm that matched it perfectly. When he came, it was with a groan against my lips.

He lifted me off of him then, flipping over onto his stomach and wrapping his arms around my thighs to pull my pussy close to his face. I watched as he lapped very delicately at my sensitive clit, bathing it gently with his tongue, using only enough pressure to build my body back up from a relaxed pleasure to an urgent desire once again. I spread my thighs wider for him and he gave a soft growl as he buried his face between my legs, dipping his tongue into my pussy to gather the moisture there, spreading it all around my folds. His thumbs held my lower lips apart, exposing me completely, and he licked my slit from bottom to top in slow strokes of his tongue. He avoided my clit for what felt like a long time, teasing me again in a way that made me almost furious.

"Travis," I said, gritting my teeth, but it was the sexiest thing I'd ever experienced being completely on edge for so long. My pussy was gushing wet, my clit throbbing each time his tongue came close or didn't touch. "Stop it."

He grinned against my pussy, tracing my clit in circles. The contact immediately made my body tense up to come but I needed more than that. It was then that I felt his fingertip tease my opening. He slipped half of one finger inside me, then pressed it all the way in. He started to curl it upward to hit that spot within me that drove me wild. He had his mouth on my pussy, sucking my clit now, his tongue stroking it in a rhythm that was making me grind my hips against his face. He slipped another finger inside me and started to pump them in and out while he tasted my clit.

My orgasm hit me again, something within me shattering as I came in his mouth. He tasted me through it, teasing my clit almost past the point I thought I could take it. He pulled his mouth away then, nuzzling my thigh with his face. He lifted his head to kiss me, slipping his tongue into my mouth to tease my own.

8

———

TRAVIS

I pulled Jenna on top of me, laying down on my back so that her head was on my chest. I stroked her soft hair, my other arm wrapped around her waist as I held her close to me. I had never experienced anything quite as sexy as Jenna sneaking into my room to fuck me in the middle of the night after that walk we'd had.

"Why did you come in here?" I asked her. She lifted her head to look at me.

"I thought that was obvious," she said with a sly smile.

"What made you decide to do it?"

She chewed on her lip. "I just couldn't stop thinking about it."

"About me?"

She nodded. "About you touching me," she paused, wanting to say more. "And also, maybe because I stalked Devinia on Instagram."

This made me laugh. "And what did you find?"

"A gorgeous model that looked perfect standing next to you."

I pulled her close to me, our bodies touching in places that drove me crazy all over again. "Jenna, look how beautiful you are lying here. It doesn't even compare," I told her, my gaze devouring her every inch.

She blushed, then said, "I think about—I think about that kiss all the time."

"Have I given you a new memory to think about?" I asked her, kissing her forehead.

"Maybe," she said teasingly, though I could feel how tight her pussy had gotten when she came, how powerful it had been. She had never come like that in her life because she had never been with me before—her body was made for mine, and I was the person who was going to get to know it inside and out.

"We'll have to try again," I said to her. I would spend hours making memories with her if it meant seeing her smile the way she was now, sweet and relaxed.

"In a minute," she said, pressing her cheek to my chest. "This is something that I've wanted for longer than I can remember."

I felt my heart palpitate at her words. It felt so good to have her in my arms after all these years. Everything was so perfect that it seemed almost too good to be true. This thought made me panic. Maybe it was.

"Tell me about this business deal you're working on." Her words pulled me from my thoughts. "You seem stressed about it."

I rubbed the stubble on my chin. "How can you tell?"

"I know you," she said. "You may have changed, but I still see glimpses of the Travis I remember."

I stared at her, smiling, and tilted my face up to kiss her. I wrapped my arms around her waist and held her against me. It felt almost like a dream, like a glimpse of the future—me and Jenna, locked in each other's arms as we were meant to be. I had never felt this way about a woman before—not before I'd met Jenna nor after we'd gone our separate ways.

"How have I changed?" I coaxed her, leaning in for another kiss.

"Nu-uh. You can't change the subject that easily. Tell me," she said, pulling her lips away from mine.

"It'll help me buy up a property I've had my eye on for a while now. It's not the biggest deal I've ever made, but it's important to me," I told her and I could see she wanted more. I sighed, "Devinia's dad is the sole investor. We made the deal before her and I broke things off." I cringed bringing her name up again, but I knew Jenna wanted honesty and I wanted to give it to her. I wanted to do right by her.

"I see," she said. "Strictly business?"

"Strictly business," I told her, giving her a peck on the cheek. "Your turn to talk. How's Yale?

"Ugh. I feel like I'm drowning," she told me. She rolled off of me then, propping herself up on her elbow to look at me from the other side of the bed. I traced her waist up and down with my fingertips, marveling in her body.

"What do you mean?"

"In work," she said, sighing as I started to trace her breasts with my fingers, not trying to arouse her but desperate to touch her soft skin. My hand trailed over her breasts, splaying over her belly as she spoke. "And debt, which is why I have to work. I don't have a minute for myself, I barely sleep—"

"You push yourself too hard," I said to her, though I could empathize with that drive to do more and be more, to improve at all times.

"I do," she agreed. "But I feel like I have to do it. There is no other option for me. School is all I'm good at."

I took her chin in my hands and tilted her face to look at me.

"That's not true," I said, staring into her green eyes, overwhelmed by her beauty, her smile, the look on her face. "You were amazing at what we just did, baby," I assured her with a wink.

This made her blush again. Her reddening cheeks lit another fire in me. I climbed down the bed, burying my face in the soft skin just below her bellybutton. I wanted to taste her again but at the same time I could live just to hear her talk. She stopped me before I could go any further. I could tell something was nagging at her.

"How do we tell Casey about this?" Jenna asked me and this sent me back into a panic. People couldn't find out about us until this deal with Devinia's father was over. If my name was seen in the press next to another woman's—even someone who meant as much to me as Jenna did—I didn't want to think about what his reaction would be. I couldn't let this deal fall through.

I rubbed at my jawline as I thought. I trusted my sister, but she had a big mouth and I couldn't risk her running it, which was a very real possibility considering how pissed she'd be once she found out about me and Jenna. I also thought about how much I didn't want to hurt Casey. I had really messed up in the past when it came to Casey's friends.

I thought back to my Sophomore year in high school. Our neighbor, who was a good friend of Casey's although she was a year or two older, could not stop hitting on me. I didn't do anything with her, but I also didn't reject the attention. I was arrogant in high school, loving the guise of popularity, and this clouded my judgment. I let Casey's friend flirt with me, and I flirted back a little. Casey overheard one day and freaked out. I thought she was just overreacting, so I didn't stop. As I got older, I kissed a couple of her friends and although I never went further, my actions really hurt Casey. I realized it soon enough, when she told me how hard it had been after dad died to make friends who just wanted to be her friend because they liked her and nothing else. I immediately stopped my flirting and focused on my studies.

But then Jenna started coming over more and more. I'd make up the guest room for her, on the weekends she'd spend with us when her mother was absent. And I'd help her with classes whenever I could. She usually didn't need it though. Jenna was way smarter than me. Friendliness turned to flirting, and eventually, I couldn't keep my eyes off of her. At my graduation party, I did it again; I kissed one of Casey's friends, her best friend. But with Jenna, it felt entirely different. The other flirty high school girls didn't hold a flame to her, but I knew Casey would see this kiss just like the rest of them. How could she not? So I freaked out and left.

"I don't think Casey will be very happy for us. She loves you, Jen. And I feel terrible for the things I put her through in school. I think we should tread lightly for a while," I told Jenna, believing the words wholeheartedly, and also realizing that it was a good excuse to keep our relationship private, just long enough for this deal to go through.

"Do you really think she'd take it that badly?" Jenna asked, tugging at the threading of the sheets.

"I just think we should be careful for a while. We need to handle this right. Casey deserves that, after everything she's been through," I said. And she did. My sister sacrificed so much for our family. She forwent her ambitions to stay in

Maplewood and care for our mother. One day soon, I hoped to make it up to her.

"You're right," Jenna said before growing quiet. I watched as she continued to anxiously fumble with her hands on top of the sheets. "I think I should go back to my room now," she told me and sauntered out without another word.

9

JENNA

I woke up in the morning with an uneasy feeling in my stomach. I was still reeling from Travis' touch, making me ache in places I hadn't experienced before. But our last conversation was what consumed most of my thoughts as I laid in bed. As amazing as the night was, I think it had been a mistake.

I looked at myself in the mirror, at my messy strawberry blonde hair and lips swollen from kissing. I looked sensual and seductive, noticeably different than usual. I felt different, too, like I had blossomed while he was inside of me, like I had become a different person. I was practically glowing as I took a shower and got dressed for the day.

I went downstairs and saw Casey sitting at the table with Alice while Travis put together a plate of food that had been arranged on a buffet at the edge of the dining room. I went over to join him and he bumped against me, giving me a secret smile as I stood next to him.

"How are you this morning?" he asked in a low voice.

"Confused," I told him honestly, daring to look up into his eyes. He glanced at my lips and I could see unease cross his face before we turned around and joined his family at the table.

"What are we doing today?" I asked.

"We're going sailing," Travis said.

"You know how to sail?"

He nodded. "I've learned throughout the years. I have a boat on the dock out back. Did you see it?"

I hadn't seen it, which meant that the property went on beyond even what I'd thought. It must have been massive if there was a whole other part of the beach that I hadn't even seen.

"Do you like sailing?" Casey asked me.

"I've never been on a sailboat before."

"You're going to love it," she said, beaming at me. The truth was that I was a little nervous to be on open water, but I refused to tell anybody that. Travis and I exchanged a couple of glances over the table but in general I avoided looking at him, afraid that my feelings would be written all over my face.

When we were finished with breakfast, we all walked to the dock together, Travis walking beside me, a little behind Casey and Alice. Our fingers touched briefly and I was reminded of how his hands felt in other places. I shivered and took a few steps away from him, afraid that if I started touching him, I wouldn't be able to stop. We got to the dock where the boat was tied up. It was small but big enough to comfortably fit all of us on deck, where there were chairs set up under an awning. Travis untied the boat and we drifted out away from the dock and further into open water. There was a nervousness in my stomach, but it all but disappeared when I saw Travis handling the boat. It was clear that he was an expert sailor who knew exactly what he was doing, and I knew I had to trust that he could keep us safe.

Once I got over my nerves, I couldn't help but notice how beautiful and peaceful it was out on the water. It was quiet, and all of us were just enjoying the sunshine and the slow rocking motion of the boat on the waves. I looked over at Travis, who was gazing over the water, and when his eyes met mine they were sparkling. I had never seen him look so happy, not even when he'd been on the phone with Casey, nor when he'd seen his parents after so long. Sailing was something that came natural to him and it made me happy when I saw him doing something he loved so much.

It was mostly quiet as we sailed, everybody enjoying the peaceful experience in their own way. I let my mind wander and take in the view. For the first time in as long as I could remember, I felt truly relaxed. Eventually, we made it to the other side of the island and Alice stood up to stretch.

"Let's stop and get something to eat," she said. "Anybody else hungry?"

"I am," said Casey, and I nodded my agreement. Travis steered us into a dock that wasn't far from what looked like a main plaza in the small town. After we docked, we got off the boat and made our way down the street toward the smell of food carts and the sound of peaceful locals chatting and going about their business. I loved it here, looking around the quaint little town. My stomach was growling and I was looking forward to getting something to eat, but I felt like I could easily spend all day wandering the town, looking around at the houses and the people who made this place their home.

We went to a swanky French restaurant in the corner of the small plaza, sitting together in a booth. I sat next to Travis, who scooted closer to me once I got settled. His thigh was touching mine, and the feeling of his body heat made my pulse race. Alice and Casey sat across from us, chatting about Alice's fiftieth. We placed our order, and after the waiter was gone, Travis' hand found my thigh. He began to brush it up and down with his fingertips, all while smiling across the table at his family.

"What do we have planned for the rest of the trip?" I asked, trying not to squirm in the booth. Travis' hand was electric on my leg, especially as he began to stroke higher, slightly parting my thighs with his hand.

"We're going snorkeling," he said, gazing at my face with a look that made me wonder how Casey didn't know what he was doing to me. I panicked for a moment, but then his fingers brushed between my legs and he started stroking up and down my clit with one knuckle, barely applying pressure. I could feel his every touch achingly through my wet panties; it felt almost as if he was touching my bare skin.

"That sounds fun," I said, trying to keep a straight face as he increased pressure between my legs.

"Have you ever been snorkeling, Jenna?" asked Alice. I shook my head, unable to speak. Travis rubbed me through my panties in slow circles, teasing my pussy. The food came and he kept his hand under the table, eating with his right hand as he slipped the other one into my panties and started stroking my bare skin. I couldn't help but to grind my hips against him, trying to be subtle as he straddled my clit with two fingers and rubbed up and down. Casey and Alice continued their conversation but I couldn't pay attention to any of it. I had stopped eating, so caught up in my pleasure that I thought if I opened my mouth I would moan aloud.

"Are you okay, Jenna?" Alice asked, a look of concern passing over her face.

"Yes," I breathed. This seemed to satisfy Alice as she directed her attention back towards Casey. I was anything but okay. I was on the verge of coming, so close that I could feel my pussy tightening. I did come when he pressed two fingers inside of me, biting hard into my lip to keep from making any noise. I was lucky that nobody was looking at me at that moment—I had no doubt that my pleasure showed on my face. It was overwhelming, especially since I couldn't move my body to respond to it like I wanted.

Travis had his eyes on me while I came, and he gave me a small smirk of satisfaction as I tried to make my body calm down. I swatted him on the knee, surprised at his daring, immensely turned on by how bold he was.

"I'm going to wash my hands," Travis said and I watched him go and he cast a glance at me over his shoulder, urging me to follow.

I opened my mouth to excuse myself, but Casey spoke first.

"So, babes. How are you liking the trip so far? Has it been the escape you needed?"

"It definitely has," I said and hoped that they couldn't see how hot my cheeks had gotten at the question. I tried not to think about how good Travis just made me feel. His touch made me forget all of my worries.

"We need to get some girl time in soon. I've been trying to give you some space to relax, but I'm growing antsy," she said jokingly.

"Case, being with you is more relaxing than pretty much anything else in my life right now. You have no idea how much I've missed you."

"I missed you too, sis," Casey smiled at my words, the look of genuine appreciation on her face. "I should have come down to visit you at Yale more. I mean it's only a two hour drive. I'm sorry I didn't."

"I'm not sure I would have been able to entertain you

anyway." I was so busy with work and classes that I never got a day off. "Besides, I could say the same. I should have come back to see you more these past four years."

"I get it, Jen. I honestly didn't expect you to ever set foot back in Maplewood again after you left for college. With your mom and everything..." Casey trailed off, but she never showed any pity in her eyes. We had both agreed to never do that to each other; pity. Both of us had been bogged down by it too much in the past.

Travis' phone buzzed twice on the table, signaling a text message. I briefly looked down, not intending to read the message until I saw Devinia's name on the screen. My eyes shot up, looking towards the bathroom, but there was no sign of Travis yet. Alice and Casey excused themselves to walk back to the beach. I told them I'd wait for Travis and meet back at the boat.

Against my better judgment, I grabbed Travis' phone and exhaled, not even realizing that I had been holding my breath. The text from Devinia was short, but it made my stomach drop.

Hey baby. Call me. Urgent business to discuss. XOXO

10

TRAVIS

After lunch, we got back on the sailboat to go to the other side of the island where we would be snorkeling. The water was even more clear over there—crystal blue and beautiful. I had gone snorkeling here the first time I came to the island and knew that my family would love it.

I watched Jenna while we were sailing, free to keep my eyes on her while my family wasn't looking. She looked beautiful with the slight wind in her hair, the sun on her golden skin, lighting up her eyes. I hadn't been able to resist touching her at lunch, although I had known I was taking a huge risk. It had been worth it to make her come, knowing that she needed to moan, needed to move but couldn't.

She didn't join me in the bathroom to continue our exchange, and she had been avoiding me ever since. I wasn't sure if she was embarrassed by her release at the table or still caught up in last night's conversation about Casey. I was more convinced than ever that we could hide our affections from my sister for the rest of the trip, especially after receiving a message from Devinia this afternoon telling me that the final paperwork signing for her father's investment would be moved up to next week. The deal was going to be finalized right after this trip was over.

When we got to the other side of the island, we tied the boat up. I helped Jenna climb out, taking her hand, and even in that brief moment I felt the connection, hot and potent between us. But something was slightly off. She met my eye while she stepped out of the boat, giving me a faint smile and nothing more as we made our way down the dock toward the kiosk where we'd rent the snorkeling gear. It was a small building, un-air conditioned with wide open windows. A girl in a bikini stood behind the rental desk, lazily reading a book.

"Hi," I said to her brightly. "We need equipment for three."

The girl gave me a bored look. "Know what you're doing?"

I nodded. She gestured behind her.

"There's stuff hanging on the wall right now. You're required by law to wear the snorkeling vest but"—she waved it off—"just do your best. Let me know if y'all need anything."

"Thanks," I said to her, and we all made our way to the back of the building. I picked out my gear, first, my eyes on Jenna. She looked confused as she surveyed the wall, and when I was finished I started pulling things off and handing them to her.

"What do I do with these?" she asked, her arms full of the snorkeling equipment. I pulled her over to the side, just so that my family was out of hearing range.

"That bikini," I said. It had been driving me crazy all day. I dared to trace her bikini line, my finger slipping just below the fabric. She was staring at me with heat and disbelief in her eyes.

"Travis," she said in a quiet voice. "You're—"

"Turn around," I said, making a spin gesture with my finger. She gave me a little shake of her head but did as I asked, allowing me a glimpse of the way her bikini bottom showed just a little bit of her round, cute ass. I looked over her shoulder to see that my sister and mother were helping each other, that neither of them were paying attention as I palmed her ass in my hands and stroking the skin outside of her bikini with my thumbs. She trembled, but pulled away quickly.

Without a word, she picked up her snorkeling gear and walked away, fastening the straps of her vest as she made her way to the beach. I had no idea what I had done to make her so upset, but I'd get to the bottom of it before the day was over. Whatever was ailing her, I wanted to make it better.

"You ready for this?" My sister asked Jenna while she hesitated at the edge of the water.

"I think so," she said. "This is slightly embarrassing, but I'm not the best swimmer. My mom never put me in lessons."

Jenna's confession made my heart ache. Her mother was never very attentive to her as she was growing up. I'm sure she had tried her best to balance a career with taking care of a daughter and I could relate to that. Balancing family time and a career was extremely difficult. Me and Casey's weekly Skype calls were my only interaction with my family these past few years, aside from holidays. Nonetheless, I couldn't help but remember all those days after school, having to set an extra place at the dinner table for a distraught Jenna, whose mom had run off to the city yet again.

"Don't worry! We've got you, girl. Travis, you're on life-guard duty!" Casey smirked at me before directing her attention back to Jenna. She splashed her best friend as they made their way deeper into the water. I took Casey's order to heart. I'd be keeping my eye on Jenna for the rest of the afternoon, ready to grab her if she needed me and selfishly ready to take in every inch of her soft, tan skin while I watched.

My mom parked herself in a chair on the beach while we dipped our faces in and out of the water, in awe of the vivid pink coral and multi-colored fishes swimming close enough to reach out and touch. Casey taught Jenna how to float on the water's surface, and Jenna picked it up quickly. I watched her drift on her stomach. Her soaked bikini bottoms clung to her skin and made me shudder with desire.

"Sea turtle!" Casey enthusiastically pointed, her smile large and beaming. This was the happiest I had seen my sister in a while.

I adjusted my snorkel and dunked my head under the soft waves to see it for myself. Through the clear water, I watched the look of wonder in Jenna's eyes as she saw the light green sea turtle wading through the reef. Elation coursed through me as I witnessed her amazement. Her and Casey both popped back up, splashing each other and laughing.

"Oh my god. Remember that turtle you almost ran over right after you got your license, Casey?" Jenna began giggling uncontrollably and Casey joined in.

"Holy crap, that was so funny! I didn't drive again for like a week. We had to bike to school with a change of clothes."

"Yeah, we were so sweaty and gross by the time we got there. We were not the best bikers," Jenna said.

"What else is new?" Casey replied, both of them tearing up at their laughter.

In their fits of giggles, Casey and Jenna had meandered into deeper waters, and the waves were getting larger. I watched Jenna's face as she looked toward the beach and realized how far away it was. Fear washed over her eyes for a brief moment, but when her gaze found me, she calmed, realizing I was there if she needed me.

Casey stared at us both for a moment with something that might have been suspicion on her face, but it was gone so quickly that I imagined it must be paranoia. Jenna tightened her life vest and motioned for Casey to swim back to the shore with her. I followed closely behind. The girls chatted the entire way back and I couldn't help but grin. Their friendship was so pure and filled with joy. I was genuinely happy that they had each other, and for a moment I felt guilt knowing that my feelings could jeopardize it. But I had to believe that their friendship was strong enough to get past anything, and that my sister could grow to be happy for me and Jenna with time.

After we snorkeled, we decided to spend the rest of the day at the beach together. We set up our chairs under an umbrella in the sand, just a few feet off the shoreline. I felt my eyes trail over Jenna as she adjusted her chair. I hadn't gotten to touch all the places I'd wanted to last night when I was in bed with her, but tonight would be different. Tonight, I was going to explore her body thoroughly. Just as soon as I figured out what was still eating at her thoughts and making her act strange everytime I tried to sneak a touch or a look.

My mom and sister were talking in their chairs as Jenna made her way back to the surf, just to dip her toes in, she said. Just watching Jenna and the way she moved turned me on, knowing what her body was capable of. She had a look of contentment on her face, one that I knew I had helped bring her in an unusually stressful time in her life. Or at least I had helped her relax up until recently. Now she tensed at my touch and I decided it was time to get to the bottom of it. With Casey and my mom distracted, I made my way to the waterline and stood next to Jenna, both of us staring out at the ocean.

"It's so peaceful. The roar of the waves," I said as I reached her.

Jenna replied with a short, "Mmm."

"My parents used to take Casey and me to the Keys when we were in grade school. I remember looking at the ocean and feeling so tiny, so insignificant. In a weird way, I think it kind of inspired me to try to be better. Like the best version of myself, you know?" Jenna finally met my eyes and nodded. Relief poured through me. "That's why I bought property out here. During the first couple years at my company, I felt pretty disconnected with my former self, and my family for that matter. I guess I was trying to chase that feeling again, to be better for them."

"I get it," her voice still held an air of hesitation and uncertainty. "I'm not even sure what the best version of myself looks like."

"You know what I think?" I asked.

"Hm?"

"I've never seen a better version of my mother than with my dad. I think your soulmate brings out the best possible you." I let those words sit with her for a moment before continuing. "I think I'm my best me when I'm with you."

Jenna let out a huge breath, like my words had just punched her in the gut.

"What's wrong, baby?" I needed an answer. I couldn't stand seeing her this way, especially if I was the cause of it.

"I saw the message from Devinia."

"Which one?" I asked.

Jenna laughed and covered her face with her palms. She brought her hands down slowly and laced them behind her small neck, looking up at the seagulls. I could tell she was growing even more frustrated.

"Gee, I don't know Travis. I think it was the one where she called you baby and signed XOXO. Does that ring a bell or do I need to specify further?" Jenna was glaring at me now and I could see the hint of betrayal in her eyes. She thought I had lied about Devinia and I's break up.

"Jenna, you don't have the full story. That text was about my business deal with her father," I pleaded for her to listen, my palms face up in front of me.

"Oh, right. Urgent business. I remember now."

"What can I do to prove it to you? I have no feelings for Devinia. The only reason I'm even still talking to her is so that her father doesn't pull out of our deal."

She paused. "So you're just stringing her along? Is that really any better?"

"Devinia knows I don't have any lingering feelings for her. I've made that very clear. Our relationship gave her a lot of publicity and she's still chasing it." When Jenna didn't respond, I continued. "I'd imagine Devinia feels as if she's flirting with a brick wall right about now. I've been extremely distracted recently," I said, reaching out to stroke Jenna's arm. She pulled away before I could make contact.

"I need to think," she told me and walked back over to Casey and my mother.

A couple of hours passed and everybody but me had fallen asleep. I walked along the beach for a few moments, thinking about work.. So far on this trip, I had been distracted by Jenna—I had barely even thought of my job. That was new for me. Work had been everything to me since I had started my business, but seeing Jenna again ignited an urgency that convinced me there were more important, sexy things to think about while I was on vacation. But now my work was beginning to affect Jenna, and not in a good way. I didn't want to think about what would happen after the trip ended and Jenna and I went our separate ways—my plan was to try and rekindle the passion we felt at the beginning of this trip and to forget about work for the time being. I'd come up with something romantic to get things with Jenna back on track and I'd enjoy the time I had left with her on this island.

11

JENNA

I sat across from Travis at dinner that night, careful not to choose the seat next to him. I knew that if he tried the same stunt he'd pulled at the restaurant, I probably wouldn't be able to hold my frustration back. I might've exploded in front of the entire table, revealing everything to Casey in the worst possible way. My night with Travis had been perfect, so satisfying and eye-opening. But ever since, I've been consistently disappointed. First at his reservations about telling Casey, which just instilled doubt in me, and now at his stupidly complicated relationship with Devinia. I wanted to believe him, that there were no lingering feelings for her. I still trembled with pleasure at his touch, and when he looked at my body, it drove me crazy. But I was realizing just how much Travis had changed since high school.

"Did you enjoy yourself today, Jenna?" Alice asked.

I nodded, smiling. "I really loved it. I feel like I could live here forever."

"One day," said Travis. I looked at him and saw sincerity in his eyes which made my chest feel a bit lighter.

"Maybe you can put us both up here, Travis," Casey said, putting her hand on my arm. "We could live as roommates."

"Cocktails every day," I said.

"And the food," she gushed. "You should get on that, bro."

He chuckled. "Any time you want to come to visit, ladies, it's yours."

"I love having a rich brother," Casey said.

"You're spoiled," he teased.

"You owe me for all the times you tormented me when I was a kid," Casey said with a grin. "You used to break the heads off of my dolls."

I laughed. "That's weird, Travis."

"She used to steal my CDs and never give them back. It was revenge."

Alice rolled her eyes. "They never really grow up," she said.

"That's not true," said Travis. He looked over at me with a hint of appreciation in his eyes. "Jenna here is all grown up."

I couldn't help but blush when he said the words, knowing that he was referring to the very grown-up things we had done together last night.

"I am," I said after a moment. "So maybe I should be the one getting spoiled."

"I wouldn't mind that," said Travis, looking back, into my eyes, and I knew that he meant every word. Maybe there were parts of the Travis I thought I knew still in there.

I felt a foot against my ankle, stroking it gently, and knew from the look on Travis' face that it was him. For some reason, that subtle, secret touch made my body feel like it was growing hot, about to burst into flames at any minute. I pulled away before I could ignite, still reeling from earlier.

He kept staring at me all through dinner, practically touching me with his roaming eyes instead. Despite my remaining confusion, I wanted to be alone with Travis. I wanted to ride him, and taste him the way he had tasted me. I couldn't take my eyes off of him and I knew that he was having the same problem as he undressed me over the table. I had briefly forgotten about my earlier reservations in that moment, and about anybody else in the room until Casey said my name. I snapped my eyes away from Travis to look at my friend.

"Jen, you wanna hang out tonight? Girl time?"

"Sure," I said with a smile, trying not to show any disappointment. I felt guilty for wanting to be with Travis so much when I was here to spend time with my best friend. Besides, he deserved to squirm a little. I could tease him way worse than Devinia. "What do you have in mind?"

She shrugged. "I just want to hang out after today, maybe watch a movie."

"Yeah, we can hang out in my room. There's a TV in there."

"Okay," she said brightly. "I'm going to go take a shower. I'll be down to your room in a few minutes."

Before Travis could try anything, I left the dining room, walking out as slowly as possible so he could get a good look, making him squirm just as intended. I went upstairs to my room and changed into a nightgown, one that was cool and light and comfortable for the weather.

Casey came down into my room a few moments later wrapped in a robe, carrying two bottles of wine. She handed the one that had already been uncorked to me and then opened one for herself, sitting beside me on the bed.

"So how are you feeling?" Casey asked. "You've seemed kind of distracted this whole trip."

"I'm just thinking about how much work I have to get done at home," I said, hoping the lie didn't show. Truthfully, I hadn't thought much of school since the moment I had seen Travis leaning over me, waking me up on the beach. It had been the last thing on my mind.

"Don't think about that," said Casey, gesturing that I should start drinking the wine. I laughed and downed a big gulp straight from the bottle, just like we used to do. She did the same, and we laid in my bed hanging out while we drank, watched the movie, and chatted.

"Do you have any guys you're working on at Yale?"

I shook my head. "I'm not—I'm not interested in having a boyfriend. Men just aren't worth it."

Casey sighed. "You're right. You're totally right. I haven't met one that is. There was somebody that I thought I might bring along on this trip but it turned out that he was married."

"He was married?" I asked.

"I didn't know about it." There was a miserable, annoyed look on her face.

"So now you're single," I said.

"Yep, and not for a lack of trying," she said, sighing, taking another long, long swig of the wine. She was more than halfway done with her bottle.

"Do you think we'll be single forever?" Casey asked, staring up at the ceiling.

"No," I said, thinking of Travis. "I hope not."

"Relationships suck." Casey's voice was beginning to slur. "I am so grateful for you, Jen. I've gone through so many guys, and plenty of friends," she said as she waved her bottle around, "But you've always been there."

I didn't know what to say. I was so grateful for Casey too, and I knew she deserved honesty from me. I opened my mouth to tell her everything. That I'd always be there for her, and that I hoped she could forgive me, but I was sort of, kind of hooking up with her brother. But before I could say anything, Casey continued.

"Ugh. I mean, after high school, being told every day that some girl liked your brother, or being constantly befriended by snakes who just used me to get to him, it was so hard to find someone I could trust. Even with guys." Now it was my turn to down my bottle of wine, drowning myself in my own guilt. "I treat dates like fricken interrogations at this point. It's not a good look on me, but I can't help it."

There was a long pause. "I want you to trust me Casey, b—"

"Oh, Jen, I do! Sooo much! Like this much!" Casey said, opening her arms wide with a sloppy grin on her face. I was beginning to feel my wine as well, holding the bottle upside down to finish it off. My face was heating up and my legs were tingling.

"I trust you too," I told her, leaving it at that. We both sat silently for some time, letting the movie play in the background, but I don't think either of us were paying attention to it. I was lost deep in my thoughts. "Casey?"

"Yeah?"

"What's, like, your biggest dream?" The room was spinning a little as I layed next to my best friend, staring at the ceiling.

"Easy. Casey's Cafe!" She yelled for the entire beach to hear. We both giggled at the outburst.

"That's a good dream. I hope it comes true," I told her honestly.

"I'm gonna make it happen, girl. No matter how long it takes." She paused. "I, I just—No, no nevermind. I can't say it." I looked over. Casey was covering her face with her hands.

"What is it?"

"I just—look no one is happier for my brother than me. My dad only had so much to leave when he died, and Travis turned it into a fortune. He saved our family. I mean, my mom was in no condition to turn our finances around. She was like," Casey trailed off, growing distracted in her drunken state.

"But," she continued, her thoughts back on track. "I just wish my dad had left some of that money for me. The coffee shop could have kept us afloat too, you know? And kept me sane!"

A lump formed in my throat. I hadn't even considered how Casey felt about not receiving any of the inheritance. I remembered Travis telling me that he wanted to make his sister happy for how much she's sacrificed.

"You should tell this to Travis. I'm sure he'd understand where you're coming from," I told her, successfully grabbing her hand after a few failed tries. Our motor functions were definitely not at their best.

"Yeah, maybe," Casey said, sheepishly laughing at our inebriated movements. "Obviously I love my bro, but he's changed a lot since he left."

"Oh, I've noticed, but he still cares about you." I didn't want to make this conversation about me, but while we were on the subject, maybe Casey knew something that could help me figure out this Devinia situation. "Speaking of Travis changing, have you met any of his model girlfriends? What's that all about anyway?" I tried to sound uninterested, like it was just drunk girl chat.

"I am so glad you brought this up!" Casey was giggling again. "Travis will deny it, but I see photos of him with new chicks all the time. I mean, he acquired quite the reputation in high school with the ladies. It would make sense that he kept it up since becoming rich."

I should have never asked. My body buzzed and my already clouded thoughts grew darker. He had told me not to believe everything I heard about his reputation, though.

"Could it just be for show? For the cameras?" I asked more for myself than anything.

"It's possible. He'd never tell me though. I think he still feels really bad for everything that went down in high school." She was referring to Travis' flirting with her persistent friends. "He won't talk about girls with me anymore. I guess I can't blame him. I did give him a pretty hard time."

"Hey, maybe tomorrow we should go cruise the island for boys! Find some hot hookups," Casey said while I digested her words.

I forced a laugh. "Maybe." It was something I would have done two or three years ago, but only for flirting. I had been carrying the torch for Travis so bright and so fast that no other man had really tempted or affected me enough to give myself to him completely.

"I doubt there's anything hip on this island," she said. "Seems like mostly rich people and old folks."

"Yeah, but rich people definitely know how to party."

"Maybe you'll meet your future husband there," Casey said. "So he can pay off all your loans."

I didn't answer her, but instead reached for the remote and turned the TV up. Casey grabbed more wine from the kitchen and we continued to drink, giggling at every little thing that happened in the stupid rom com we were watching. I tried to take my mind off of Travis and enjoy the time I had with my best friend. It was good to see Casey so happy; she hadn't always been this way. But, despite her obstacles, she had blossomed into someone with sheer confidence, the life of the party in any room.

I turned the TV off once Casey's snoring was loud enough to overpower it. I rolled over, staring at the door while I thought about Travis. I knew how important his work was to him. He had built a million-dollar business and he had every right to be proud of it. This deal with Devinia's dad was just another means to his success. I could be ok with that, but I needed to make sure his relationship with her really was nothing more, and that this reputation of his was just rumors and lies.

I pushed the covers back, unable to process my thoughts in my room that now smelled like stale booze. I stumbled to the door, still a little tipsy and made my way into the hall. The house had a blue hue to it at this hour, everything covered in moving shadows, reflections of the waves outside. Family photos hung in tasteful arrangements all through the long hallway. One photo depicted the entire family, before their father had passed. I looked at their smiling faces, Travis' arms wrapped around Casey in a sweet brotherly embrace. I was happy to find that I made the family photo wall as well. There was a picture of me and Casey at the sleepaway camp we had spent many summers at. Another was of us at Casey's sixteenth birthday. She rented out an entire bowling alley even though none of our friend group even knew how to hold a bowling ball.

I stopped at a familiar photo. I had long, straightened hair and a full face of makeup. I remembered getting ready that day, putting so much time into my appearance out of nerves and anticipation. Travis stood next to me, effortlessly handsome in his black graduation cap and robe. I could still feel his hand lightly rubbing my back as we posed, teasing me like he often did. My younger self was almost as wrought with desire as I have been on this trip. My heart sank at a sudden realization as I studied the framed moment. This photo had been taken less than an hour before he kissed me and left. I never saw him in person again until a week ago.

No longer able to bear the memory, I kept walking, meandering past several guest rooms, before choosing the most colorful one to explore. I honestly wasn't even sure how many bedrooms were in this house, but this room was painted in a coral pink, the vibrant shade of the reef we had explored today. There was an enormous king sized bed in it and an on suite bathroom that was completely stocked with toiletries. It was bigger than most homes' master bedrooms, but Travis had insisted Alice take the master on this trip, which I knew was down the hall. This room must be for important guests, maybe Travis' business partner, who he said had helped buy this property.

Curious, I pulled open several drawers on the wooden dresser. My heart sank as I stared into the open top drawer. In it was a black lace thong and a matching bra. My heart began beating fast and I couldn't see straight, the room growing blurrier than it already had been from the wine. I recognized this lingerie. It was the same lacey bra and panties that Devinia had been wearing in that photo on her Instagram.

I grabbed the panties before slamming the drawer shut. I stormed down the hallway, feeling the confidence that too much wine brought me. My feet stopped in front of a familiar closed door, Travis' room. I didn't knock, just barged in without a second thought. Travis was lying in bed, naked from the waist up. His comforter was pushed to the end of the bed and his sheets were in disarray. He looked frustrated as I studied his face, and I wondered if it was because of the conversation we had earlier.

"Jenna? What are you do—" He stopped as his eyes found the lacey black evidence that I was now holding in a death grip, the whites of my knuckles showing.

"Is this part of that urgent business Devinia had mentioned earlier?" I shook the thong in front of me, tears forming in my eyes.

"Jenna, please let me explain." Travis scurried out of bed and stood before me.

"I think you've done enough of that, Travis!" I tried to walk away, but he grabbed my wrist and spun me back to him, his expression pleading.

"Jenna, it's not what you think. Please."

No matter how angry I was, no matter how hard I tried —and I tried very hard in that moment—I couldn't say no to those beautiful hazel eyes, filled with regret and sadness. I nodded, allowing him to go on.

Travis grabbed my free hand. "Those are Devinia's. I won't deny it." My heart sunk to the depths of my stomach. "But, hear me out. We did date. I have been very open with you about that. And after a very uneventful relationship, we broke up. Just like I told you. I must've missed those when I was moving her things out." He motioned to the panties, stinging my hand.

"So, she was here?" There was no reason Travis wouldn't bring his gorgeous girlfriend to his private island, but something in me felt betrayed by it. After all of the kisses and stolen touches we'd shared here, it felt like ours, like Devinia was an intruder. But now I was starting to think that I was the intruder.

"For a couple photo shoots, yeah. It was never much of a vacation. Even when we were dating, our time was mostly spent working. She loved getting professional shots with me in front of the camera, to show her rich boyfriend off to the world. And I suppose the beach made a good backdrop." Travis rolled his eyes then looked at the floor, ashamed at his admissions. "I'm sorry I keep hurting you. But those were an honest mistake. They should have been thrown away a long time ago."

I looked down at the lingerie still in my hand. "I'm just trying to figure this all out. My feelings and how they fit into your world, I mean. It seems like everything is keeping us apart. Casey, Devinia, your job," I trailed off, a tear escaping me.

Travis wiped it away with his thumb. "I need you to trust me. Nothing can keep us apart if we don't let it."

Still a little tipsy, but entirely sure of myself, I looked into his eyes. "I do trust you," I said.

More tears fell down my face now and Travis caught them with his kisses, tasting the salt on my cheeks. He put his hands on my waist, pulling me against him as he took my mouth in a slow, relishing kiss. He began kissing my neck then. The touch of his lips on my sensitive skin spread pleasure throughout my body. Suddenly, I hiccuped and let out a chuckle.

"I'm a little drunk," I told him, a shy smile on my face. Amusement danced in his eyes, and a bit of mischief.

"Let's get you to bed then." In one swoop, he picked me up beneath my knees and threw me over his shoulder.

"Travis!" I shrieked. He carried me out of his room and down the hallway towards my bedroom. I began to panic when I realized where we were headed, and who was still in there.

"Travis, wait! Casey's asleep in there," I told him in an urgent whisper. He nodded and put his finger to his lips with a wink.

Slowly, Travis opened the door, silently tip-toeing in

with me still over his shoulder. His hand had found a comfortable position on my ass, and he squeezed it as reassurance. My heart leaped. He gently lowered me onto the other side of the bed from where Casey had fallen into a deep sleep, snoring softly now. He gave me a peck on the check, lingering for just a moment.

"Goodnight," he whispered. I clung to his hand, not wanting to see him go, though I knew he had to. "I'll see you tomorrow. I have something special planned," he comforted me with one more kiss to my lips.

"Goodnight," I said, and closed my eyes as he left. Travis was running through my mind, not only his touch but the fact that it seemed like he was genuinely interested in being with me. I was still a little hesitant, though. I had no doubt that we could tell Casey soon, and she'd find a way to be happy for us. Our girl time today had further confirmed how permanent our friendship really was. But I still had some doubt about Travis' new life and if I really did fit within it. I had said that I trusted him, and I meant it, but I didn't want to be Devinia's shadow, or worse, overshadowed by his work.

12

TRAVIS

The next day, my eyes were on Jenna consistently. I couldn't stop looking at her, though the threat of it being noticed by my family was a real risk that I shouldn't have been willing to take. Still, it felt worth it to look her over, drink her in even when she wasn't watching. Her eyes often found mine, though, and I could tell that she was thinking just what I had been thinking. We'd spent most of the day together just relaxing at the beach and things had built up between us, especially when Casey went back up to the house to use the restroom, leaving me alone in the water with Jenna. I stroked her thighs, touched her pussy through the outside of her bikini as I dared to sneak a kiss that couldn't last as long as I wanted it to.

I turned to Casey as we walked up the beach. "So, Case, there's someone I was thinking of inviting over tonight who I think you might find interesting."

Casey exchanged a glance with Jenna, who had her eyebrows raised. I had a feeling Jenna knew that something was up, though I hadn't made plans with her earlier in the day. I had something private and personal ready for later tonight, something that I knew Jenna would never forget.

"Oh yeah?" asked Casey. "Who?"

"A friend of mine. Very rich, good-looking, loves pretty girls. He lives just off the island."

"Sounds like my type," said Casey, almost gushing already. "Is he smart?"

"He graduated top of the class at Harvard," I said. I knew that I was feeding right into what she wanted. The plan was to distract her with Jack so that I would have time to sneak off with Jenna later that night. I hoped that it would work—I didn't think I could go another night without touching her.

"Perfect," Casey said. "What do you think, Jen?"

"I think you need to get laid," Jenna said, and Casey laughed while I rolled my eyes. That particular part of Casey's plans was something that I did not under any circumstances ever want to hear about.

Jenna continued, "Seriously though, you should go out and have some fun, Casey. You deserve this."

"So should I give him a call?" I asked her, knowing the answer already.

"Yes," said Casey, and she and Jenna went ahead of me as I pulled out my phone. I waited until I heard their voices dissolve to dial the number.

"Hey, Jack," I said when he answered the phone.

"Hey, man," said Jack. He was a good guy, always friendly, otherwise I wouldn't be setting him up with my sister.

"You know how you've been talking about wanting to meet my sister?"

"Yes," Jack said, his voice immediately perking up. He had seen my sister once and had carried a thing for her since.

"Want to come over tonight? I can introduce you two. Have a few drinks, get to know her."

"Sure," said Jack, and I was thankful again that he was always down to have a good time. We made plans for him to come to my house in about an hour, and by the time I got upstairs the girls were showering after having been at the beach and my mother had already retreated to her room for the night.

We all went downstairs, me behind Jenna with my hand on her waist, guiding her subtly just so that she could feel the heat of my skin there. We sat down on the couches until the doorbell rang. I got up to answer it and greeted my friend Jack. I clapped him on the back, inviting him inside. Casey stood up when he walked in.

"Casey, this is Jack," I said, and I saw the look on her face before she even shook his hand. I had done good—I knew my sister very well, and Jack was just her type.

"Casey," said Jack with a charming smile, sitting down next to her on the couch. They started to talk and I glanced over at Jenna, gesturing for her to meet me in the dining room.

"We're going to get some water," I said to Jack and Casey, who didn't even look over at me. I got up and followed Jenna into the kitchen, where I took her hips in my hands and pulled her against me. I kissed her once, then twice, each kiss growing deeper. I couldn't help but to taste her mouth, to tease her tongue with mine.

"You should say you're tired and go to bed early."

"Why?" she asked.

"Because I'm trying to leave them alone. Go up to your room and wait. I'll be up there soon."

"But if Casey's still awake, we can't—"

"I'm going to try to convince them to go out," I said with

another kiss. She nodded then and we left the kitchen, going back outside to the living room where Casey and Jack were sitting even closer than before. I took one look at them and knew that I was going to have no trouble convincing them to go for a night out together.

"I'm really tired," Jenna said from behind me, yawning and stretching in a way that made her body look lean and limber. "I think I'll go to bed."

"Goodnight," said Casey, without even looking away from Jack. I sat down on the couch with them but they were distracted with each other. I was eager to get them out of the house.

"Why don't you guys go out tonight?" I asked them. "There's that new bar—"

"I've been wanting to try that place since we got here," Casey said, filling me with relief that she caught on so quickly. "Would you want to go?"

"Sure," said Jack. "Let's have a couple more drinks first and we're out."

"Okay," said Casey.

"Okay, guys," I said, unable to wait. I was going to start my plans for my night with Jenna now, whether they were lingering or not. "I'm going upstairs."

"No problem," said Casey, her voice dreamy, and I disappeared around the corner. Instead of going upstairs, though, I dipped through the back hallway that led to the side door of the house. I closed it quietly behind me and looked around outside. There was a window I had crawled through a few times when I'd locked myself out that I knew led directly into her bedroom. I started to climb the lattice, careful not to put too much pressure on any of my limbs, and lifted myself onto the roof. Then I sat outside her window, tapping on it with the backs of my knuckles. There was a sheer curtain covering the window but I could see her outline through the creamy, opaque fabric. I laughed when I saw her scramble off the bed before she came over to the window, pulling the curtain aside.

When she saw me, she smiled, opening the window.

"What are you doing?" she asked, putting her hands on her hips.

"I was going to wait until they left for their date but I can't wait any longer, so I'm sneaking you out."

She looked at me with playful amusement in her eyes.

"Okay," she said. I climbed back out the window and helped her through, then we slid down the roof until we got to the bottom ledge. I held onto her hand as she swung down to the lattice, scaling it to the ground. I climbed about halfway and dropped, then wiped off my knees and took her hand as we started in the direction of the alcove I had set up for her earlier that day. It was a private place, my favorite on the island, and I had a feeling that the beauty of it would take Jenna's breath away just like I wanted it to.

"Where are we going?" she asked. I looked over at her as we walked, pressing through a thatch of trees that led to the private alcove.

"It's a surprise," I said. I took her hand once I knew that we were past the safety of the trees and laced our fingers, glancing over at her face just to see that smile I knew I'd put there. We walked for a few moments in silence, picking through the trees in some places until we came upon a narrow path that squeezed between two rocks. I slipped between them into the alcove and she followed me, looking around in wonder at the private area of the beach and the hanging rock that would shelter our fire. There was a blanket set up in the alcove on the sand, as well as a cooler with a bottle of champagne and fresh fruit inside.

"You can go sit in there," I said to her as she looked around in wonder. "I'll light a fire."

She nodded, going into the alcove. Instead of sitting down, she looked around at the stone walls, tracing her finger along the smooth rock as if it was unlike anything she'd ever seen before. I began to build the fire, carrying out some of the wood I had brought in that morning when I'd planned this surprise picnic. As soon as I had a fire going, I stood up to see that Jenna had moved closer to the shore and was sitting in the sand, her bare feet being lapped by the water. She was so beautiful in the light of the moon and the shine of the stars that I thought, for a moment, I would never be able to look away from her. I thought she was perfect.

13

JENNA

Travis sat down next to me at the beach while I gazed at the sky, filled with bright stars that twinkled and flickered on a cloudless night. We were far away from the lights of the house and the town on the island; nothing obscured the view of the stars' brightness. The whole moment was perfect, especially when Travis put his hand over mine in the sand. He began to stroke my skin with the pad of his thumb, rubbing in slow circles that teased with little effort. Even that touch of his hand after the past couple of days was enough to make me squirm on the sand. I turned my face to look at him and saw that he was staring at me with an intent look in his eyes.

"What are you thinking?" he asked me.

"That I want to write about this," I said, gesturing to the beautiful night sky and the pristine alcove. Travis smiled.

"What are you thinking?" I asked him, my voice trembling from that simple, sensual touch of his hand. He tilted his face close to mine, taking my bottom lip between his.

"All of these years I've thought about you," he said. "I always wished—I wished that we had met later."

"I can't believe you had a crush on me," I said, remembering all over again our first sweet kiss.

"I can't believe I didn't tell you. We wasted years without each other."

"I have to admit, you running away afterwards...It felt like my mom all over again, but in a way it hurt worse," I didn't want to ruin our romantic moment, but I've been needing to say this for a while now.

He leaned in to kiss me again, a soft kiss that promised more. He kept the promise by placing his hand on my cheek, pulling me closer as he slipped his tongue into my mouth to coax mine. I responded in full, my hands in his hair, and suddenly he was standing up and lifting me with him. He carried me back to the alcove where the large blanket was set up and dusted the sand off of my body with his hands, focusing in particular on my ass. He dusted himself off as well and then sat down on the blanket, pulling me down so that I was lying next to him.

"I'll never leave you again. I want to make up for all the time we've lost," he said, looking down at my body, tracing between my breasts with his fingers. "I don't think I'll be able to stop once I start."

"I don't want you to stop," I breathed, tilting my face up to bite his bottom lip. My hands worked to unbutton his shirt as I spoke and he shrugged out of it, his body magnificent and perfect in the light of the fire and the moon. "I want you to fuck me forever, Travis."

He gave a soft growl and pulled my dress up without hesitation, pulling it off of my shoulders. I was naked for him, my heavy breasts swollen and sensitive, pussy hot with longing. He studied my body with half-lidded eyes, his fingers pinching my nipples gently, circling around them until they grew even harder. His hand trailed down my body, fingers tracing my belly button before lowering to toy with the small patch of curls just above my clit. He ran his fingers through it, watching my face as I lifted my hips to get more from him.

Travis leaned in then, putting his lips to my ear as his fingertip started to stroke my bud in just the right way.

"I'm taking my time with you tonight, baby," he said in a soft, velvety voice as he straddled my clit with two fingers and rubbed it up and down. My eyes rolled with pleasure, my hips moving against his hand.

"Travis, I don't think—"

"I think you can handle it," he said with a grin, kissing me deeply as he moved his body over mine. He started at my neck, planting hot, open-mouthed kisses all along the skin there, occasionally nipping just to cause little jolts of pain that spread through my body, down to my needy pussy. His fingers teased me relentlessly, only occasionally touching my clit as he dipped his finger into me to gather the moisture from the source. He slipped a finger inside of me halfway and started to pump it in and out, never going deeper, just taunting me by pleasuring my opening. I went wild underneath him already, breathless.

"This isn't fair," I said when he had dipped two fingers fully inside me but pulled them out just as he was giving me pleasure.

"You're gonna come so hard when I'm done with you," he said softly, his lips latching onto one of my nipples and sucking on it as he rubbed my clit with his thumb. His tongue lapped at the hard bud before he switched to the other breasts, stroking only the outside of my pussy lips in soft brushes of his fingers.

When he was done sucking my breasts, he finished his

descent down my body, his mouth hovering between my legs.

He swept his tongue from the bottom of my slit to the top, focusing on my clit when he got there. He only licked me for a few moments before he broke, starting to devour me as I bucked against his face. To my dismay, he held my hips still as he sucked and licked my pussy, tormenting me by not letting me move. Each sweep of his tongue got me closer to coming, and I was squirming as hard as I could against his hands as my pussy started to clench and throb. He must have felt it, because he pulled away at the last second, a sly smile on his face as he lifted it to look at me. I pouted at him, flustered and angry.

"Poor baby," he said, crawling up my body to kiss me. "Are you ready to be fucked now? Is that what you need?"

I nodded, desperate for nothing less. He reached over into the bag and pulled out a wrapper, ripping it open and sliding the condom down his length. Then he put his hands on my knees and held them apart, looking into my eyes as he slid his cock into me without even having to guide it. My mouth was open in a silent whimper as he filled me up and began to grind against the back of my pussy, slowly moving his hips back and forth. Occasionally, he would pull all the way out of me and rub the head of his soaking wet cock back and forth over my slit, making sure to touch my clit with it each time. It sent a lick of pleasure through me that was almost intolerable in how brief it was.

"Stop it," I begged, wrapping my hand desperately around him to guide him back inside of me. I craved that feeling the moment he stopped every time and it was starting to feel like I couldn't take it anymore, couldn't stand the teasing.

He shook his head, grinning as he stopped my hand

with his. He pinned my hands over my head on the blanket, sliding back inside of me effortlessly and starting to fuck me in a way that was painfully slow. He moved with elegance, his hips in the perfect motion to make me absolutely crazy. I writhed on the blanket but couldn't pull my hands away from his strong grip. He rode me in long, languid strokes.

"I need more," I begged him.

"Not now, baby," he said, grinding inside of me. "Be patient, my love."

His words made me feel light, even as he tortured me with his slow movements. I raised my hips to meet his, glad that he couldn't stop me. I tried to move more quickly, and take him deeper and harder, but each time he would pull his hips away completely, leaving me empty and nearly on the verge of frustrated tears. I stopped moving then, knowing that he was trying to teach me a lesson. This was his game, and he was going to be thorough. My pleasure only built as he rode against me, especially when he reached down and started to rub my clit in slow circles. He touched it in a way that made me squirm from him, the pleasure so intense that I could barely take it. It didn't work —he touched me anyway, making me moan loudly as the feeling overwhelmed my entire body.

"I'm going to come, Travis," I said, unable to quit bucking my hips now.

"No, you're not," he said, speeding his hips up. I whimpered as he gave me what I wanted, but he pulled out at the very last minute, making me whine with a frustration that was almost painful.

"Please," I said in barely a whisper. He leaned down to kiss me, then sighed against my lips and let go of my hands. Instead, he wrapped my legs around his hips and put his hands on my ass to hold me still while he slid back inside of me. This time, he didn't go slow. He didn't hold my hands, either, but used his own to bounce my hips against his while he fucked me hard and deep. He was still going slow, but it was more than satisfying to feel him hitting the very back of my pussy in strokes that seemed to claim me entirely.

Finally, he sped his hips up until he was truly fucking me on the blanket. My nails were digging into his back as he pounded into me, his mouth crushed against mine to muffle both of our cries. He reached down to rub my clit with his fingers, and this time he allowed my orgasm to build.

"Please let me come," I said before he could stop, holding him close with my legs around his hips. He continued to fuck me, hard and fast.

"Do it, baby. Come for me," he said in a low voice. I bit into his lip, my whole body seeming to throb as I let go and came in a crash against his body. I couldn't help but cry out in a loud voice and I hoped no one at the house overheard. I shuddered underneath him and felt him come, too, as the throbbing of my pussy brought him over the edge. His body collapsed on top of mine, warm and inviting as he pulled out of my pussy. We were quiet as we caught our breath, but then he kissed me, looking into my eyes.

"I've never met anyone like you, Jenna," he said, stroking my lips with his fingers. "I never thought I would again after I let you go. I hope you realize, no one could compare to you in my eyes. No one has made me feel even close to how I feel with you."

I kissed his fingers, tracing his back with my hands. "You found me," I said, kissing him softly. He smiled, nodded, and rolled over so that he could pull me onto his chest. I found myself dozing and forced my eyes to stay open.

"And I won't let go this time. My obligations to my family were pulling me in a different direction in high school, and I had to prioritize them. I hope you understand. But now nothing is keeping us apart, baby."

I understood. I admired the way he took care of his family, in a way my parents could never take care of me. "Thanks for looking out for me Travis, always."

I rested my head on his warm, chiseled muscles, letting myself relax and he nuzzled up against me.

"Always," he said.

"Can't fall asleep," I said groggily. "We need to go back to the house."

"We will in a minute." Travis was petting my hair. "Just a minute, Jen."

14

TRAVIS

I woke up and looked around. It took me a moment to realize that we were still in the alcove, which was shading us from the bright light of the morning sun. Jenna was laying on my chest, and I shook her gently awake.

"Jenna," I said, stroking her arm with my fingers. "Baby, wake up. We fell asleep."

She stirred, blinking at me, and after a moment her eyes went wide in panic and she scrambled to her feet, grabbing her dress and throwing it on. I felt panicky myself as I got dressed. I hadn't meant to fall asleep with her there but it had been so comfortable and warm, such a perfect moment after I got to make love to her and tease her pussy. I had gotten comfortable and drifted off, and now we were stuck outside with no excuse as to why we were together so early in the morning.

"God, I can't believe we fell asleep here," Jenna said, running her hands through her hair. "I don't know what to do. This is not the best way for Casey to find out."

"Go up to the house first," I told her. "I'll follow later from the other door."

"Okay," she said, biting her lip. She leaned in to kiss me then, wrapping her arms around my neck. There was a smile on her lips that made me feel relieved—she was nervous, but she didn't seem to regret the night before.

"Last night was perfect," she said, confirming my thoughts. I kissed her again, nuzzling her cheek.

"It was," I said. "We'll repeat it later. I'll see you in a bit."

She kissed me one more time and then disappeared through the narrow tunnel between the rocks. I waited for about twenty minutes, folding up the blanket and putting the cooler away to carry in later. I wanted to make it look like I had just gotten up in the morning to take a walk, rather than the fact that I had slept outside.

I started to make my way back to the house, following the outer perimeter of the property to go in through the servant's entrance. I walked up to the house, pushing in through the door that led to a dark hallway. I flipped on the light switch and at that moment, the adjacent door opened, and the cook was standing there. She gave me a puzzled look but I only smiled at her and kept walking, hoping she wouldn't say anything to anybody.

I went upstairs and undressed, stepping into the shower. I regretted washing the scent of Jenna off of me. The blend of her sex and her perfume was a heady one, something that I could breathe in all day and be satisfied. In the shower, I thought of Jenna, smiling as I pictured that look on her face when I was teasing her. One of the best parts was hearing her say the word 'please' in that sweet little voice, then giving her what she desperately wanted while she moaned and bucked against me. It wasn't only that—not just the sex

—but seeing Jenna's smile was something that made me feel almost weak.

Once I got out of the shower, my phone rang. It was my business partner Arthur. I got dressed and made my way to the beach, where I could talk to him safely out of earshot from my family.

"Hey, bro! How's the vacation treating you?" Arthur answered.

"Hey, man. Sorry I missed your first call. It's going really great," I told him and he detected the smile on my face.

"You got laid, didn't you? Your sister's friend finally give in?"

"More like we both did. She's amazing, Arthur."

"Damn. So this is more than just a fling, then?"

"I think so," my smile now coated my entire face and my pulse quickened at the thought of Jenna in my arms forever.

"I'm happy for you man, really. But a word of advice: don't let Devinia's dad catch wind of it until the papers have been signed," Arthur said on the other end.

"Yeah, I've given that a lot of thought. I haven't even told Casey about us yet. It's our little secret until the deal goes through. Casey will understand once I can explain everything."

"For sure. That's actually why I called. Did Devinia tell you the signing got moved up?"

"In a few words," I said, remembering her obnoxiously flirtatious text that got me in trouble with Jen. "Two days from now. I can be back by then. I can't wait to get this thing done and over with."

"Me too. Devinia and her dad have been a real pain in my ass."

"Tell me about it."

Arthur proceeded to fill me in on all of the work that

needed to be done before the signing on Monday. It would take me all day, but the results would be well worth it. No more playing nice to Devinia, and I could finally secure one of the most important deals I've ever made.

After texting my family and Jenna that I had a work emergency, I spent the rest of the day in town, at the warehouse building that I had transformed into my own personal office so I could still get things done in peace while on the island. I had plenty of desk space back at the house, but I knew I wouldn't be able to focus there. I'd feel guilty for being so close to Jenna, but not able to spend time with her. I'd let the girls have a fun day to themselves while I got some important work done in regards to my upcoming deal. My heart rate shot up just at the thought of it. It would be life changing, but I needed some time to focus on my work in order to make it happen. I felt like I had been dropping the ball a bit on this trip, blissfully distracted by Jenna's company.

Later, a call from Jack pulled me from my computer screen. I checked the time before I answered; it was already six. I'd almost finished everything I needed to get done, just in time to head back for dinner.

"Hey man, what's up?" I greeted Jack packing my things up and making my way back to the beach that would lead me home.

"Travis, what the hell bro? You said your sister was into me!" Jack sounded upset.

"She totally was. What happened?"

"She spent the entire night complaining about you, man. Travis has so much money. Travis works so hard. Travis has so many girls flaunting over him," he attempted to mimic Casey's voice. "I could barely get a word in."

"Shit. I'm sorry, Jack. I had no idea." What had come

over Casey? Jack was an amazing guy and she ruined what could have been an amazing date. Over...me? I thought I had made it clear that it was all for her: my job, me putting up with models like Devinia, me moving to LA. I did it to help our family.

"You should definitely talk to her, bro. I would love to go on another date. She's crazy hot and I think she's really funny, but you two have some things to figure out first."

"Will do. Again, I'm really sorry."

"Alright. Talk to you later, man."

I hung up feeling deflated. I kicked a pile of sand and then quickly shut my eyes when it blew back into my face. As I got closer to the house, I saw a familiar slender figure in the distance, sitting in front of the ocean with her legs clutched. I made my way to her.

15

JENNA

$\mathcal{I}$ snuck back into the house through the sliding back doors, hoping that Casey and Alice were still getting ready for breakfast in their rooms. There was no sign of anyone as I crept in, aside from a few cooks preparing breakfast in the kitchen. I smiled at them as I passed, cautiously making my way up to my room.

I huffed, leaning up against my bedroom door behind me. My bed was still made, no sign of being slept in last night. I just had to hope that Casey's date went well enough that she hadn't noticed my absence.

I quickly changed into new clothes and washed yesterday's makeup off. In the mirror, I looked like a new woman. I seemed to glow after every nightly encounter with Travis. The thought of him teasing me last night before giving me the most amazing release of my life made me blush.

I waited until my bright red cheeks faded and my heart rate relaxed a little before heading down for breakfast. Casey and Alice were already seated next to one another at the beautifully set table. Four placemats were out, but Travis was missing.

"Good morning, Jenna. How did you sleep?" Alice greeted me. Casey huffed as she sipped her drink.

"Um, very well. Thanks," I responded and looked at Casey. She refused to make eye contact with me, twirling the mimosa in her champagne chute. We sat for a few moments, me trying to catch her eye and her clearly avoiding me.

Alice got up to grab coffee from the kitchen, and I followed her, wanting to escape my hostile best friend, who may or may not know I've been sleeping with her brother.

"Thank you again for coming on this trip, Jenna. I know Travis and Casey have cherished it so much. As have I," Alice said, looking at me with such warmth.

"Well, thank you for having me. And for taking such good care of me," I added. Alice knew I meant more than just on this trip. That I was so grateful to have had her as a mother figure in my life.

"I'm just so glad that Casey has you." Tears began to well in Alice's eyes. "I don't mean to get emotional, but after her father died, Casey really struggled with letting people in. That all changed with you."

"She's done the same for me. Casey has really been a rock," I told Alice, feeling guiltier than ever for not coming clean with my best friend sooner.

"She's such a strong girl, isn't she?" Alice's eyes were on Casey now, who was looking out the windows at the ocean, deep in thought. "I just worry that I've held her back in my grief. She deserves so much more."

"I don't think Casey regrets a thing about staying in Maplewood. You're right. She's strong and so ambitious. She'll be okay," I told Alice, trying to convince myself too.

Alice gave me a hug before we went back to the table with our coffees.

"Does anyone know where Travis was last night? I

walked by his room around midnight on my way for some water and he wasn't there," Alice asked as we sat back down.

I swallowed hard, glancing away from them. I hoped they wouldn't see the guilt written on my face.

"I have no idea," I said. "I went to bed early."

"You went to bed really early," Casey agreed, studying my face. "Are you feeling okay?"

I couldn't meet her eyes, but looked at my food instead.

"I just felt really worn out last night. The sun makes me tired."

"I bet," said Casey. There was something in her voice that made me anxious, paranoid that she knew about Travis and I. When I looked at her face, there was a placid smile on it, though this smile didn't reach her eyes, which were staring daggers at me now.

"How was your date?" I asked, trying to change the subject. I hoped they would just let it go, that nobody would ask about Travis again. I felt like every time somebody brought it up I blushed. Thinking about Travis made me hot no matter what, especially after what he had done to me last night. I had been teased past my breaking point and come so hard that it had taken my breath away.

"It was okay," Casey said shortly. "I don't want to talk about it."

"Why not?" I asked.

"Because this is my mom's birthday," she said, her voice on the edge of snapping at me. "That's what we should be focused on. All of us."

I felt guilt run through me again but tried to hide it from my face.

"You can talk about it, honey," said Alice. "I want to hear about it."

"It's not a big deal," Casey protested. "I don't need to talk about it."

"Okay," I said. I felt something in my gut, a lump that had formed there when I'd noticed Casey's mood then grew even larger after my conversation with Alice. I felt guilty for not being there for Casey, for not asking her privately about her date. I felt guilty, also, because I knew how she would feel about the night I'd spent with her brother. "I just—"

"Maybe if you were in bed last night like you had said, then you'd know how my date went." Casey's eyes were filled with betrayal as she gave me a pained look.

"Casey—"

"Save it. I saw you coming back this morning, wearing the same clothes from last night. And just a little later, I saw Travis do the same." Casey looked like she wanted to cry, but she was too angry to do so. "I shouldn't have been surprised. You two have been exchanging weird looks this entire trip."

"Wait, what are you saying, Casey?" Alice was shocked, and shared a similar look of betrayal in her own eyes.

"Her and Travis are totally hooking up. Aren't you, Jen?"

"I, I mean—we," I fumbled with my words until it all came rushing out. The truth flooded through me, and I hoped it would wash the guilt away with it. "Yes. We snuck out last night to go on a date. We genuinely wanted you and Jack to hit it off, but we were also kind of hoping that he'd distract you a bit." When I said it out loud it sounded so selfish.

Casey scoffed, rolling her eyes before looking back out to the ocean. I looked to the stairs in desperation, hoping Travis would come strolling down to help me dig my way out of this mess. But he didn't show. He was dealing with a "work emergency" as he put it. He always seemed to be dealing with one of those. I had to deal with this blow on my own.

I decided that I was going to tell Casey everything, knowing it was the only way I could attempt to earn back the trust I had lost. "Remember Travis' graduation party?" I addressed both Casey and Alice. "We kissed. And then he left and I thought it was over."

If the look Casey had given me before wasn't betrayal, this one sure as hell was.

"High school?" Now Casey began to cry. She wiped the tears from her cheeks as Alice rubbed her back. I had betrayed them both. She didn't need to say it; I knew I had broken our pact. I had resurfaced all of the insecurities Casey felt in school, her friends that used her to get to Travis. I wasn't like those friends, and I had to prove that to her.

"I'm so so sorry Casey. I never meant to hurt you, but we both have feelings for each other," I tried to convince her that this was different. "We were planning on telling you, but it's still new and we wanted to do it right."

Casey responded slowly, looking up at me with glossy eyes. "I needed you last night. And I needed my brother on this trip. I've barely gotten to see him since he left for LA. I've missed him, but he's been so distracted these past few days. And now I know why."

I looked down at my shaking hands, tears forming in my own eyes. We had really hurt Casey, and I wasn't sure how I could possibly make up for it.

"I can't say that I would have reacted perfectly if you had just been honest with me from the start, but it would have been better than hiding it from me. I didn't know exactly what secret you two were keeping from me on this trip, but all those whispers and weird looks? I noticed them, and they really hurt. It all really hurts."

"I know, Casey. It was so wrong of us. How can I make it right?"

"I don't know, Jen," Casey had stopped looking at me. She pulled her chair out and went upstairs, not looking back.

Alice kept her gaze on the placemat in front of her. "She just needs some time to process, hun. I think we both do." She rested her hand on top of mine before following her daughter upstairs. I put both hands to my face and sobbed for what seemed like hours.

16

TRAVIS

She was sitting on the beach, staring at the horizon when I came up behind her. She shivered, the air now cold with a breeze coming off the sea. The sun was about to set, so the coast held a purplish hue to it, ready to embrace nightfall.

"Hi, baby," I said, sitting by her side. She tensed at my words and when she finally looked at me, I saw that her green eyes were red around the edges, bloodshot, and her cheeks were puffy. She had been crying for a while. My heart sank. I put my arm around her shoulders to try and stifle the shivering. "Hey, what's wrong?"

"Where have you been all day?" She asked me.

"Working. I told you that, " I said carefully, unsure how that could have caused this response. "My deal is about to go through. I've had a lot to do to prepare for it, but I thought about you all day." I made circular motions on her lower back, coaxing her to tell me more.

"Casey knows," she sobbed after a few moments of silence. Her hands covered her face as her slender frame shook from the tears. "And your mom knows. Casey figured it out and they hate me now. I think—I think I ruined my friendship with Casey."

"Jen, I'm so sorry I wasn't there. Why didn't you call me?"

"It felt wrong to tell you over text. I wanted to tell you in person. I—I wanted you to comfort me in person."

My heart broke. I felt like I had royally screwed up, and seeing Jenna so distraught was killing me.

"They don't hate you, Jen. They could never hate you. We'll make things right. We'll plan an amazing day tomorrow. I'll arrange a helicopter ride or charter a submarine. We'll get everyone together and explain everything. Once Casey sees how happy we are together, she won't be able to stay ma—"

"You can't fix everything with money, Travis," Jenna's words held a fierceness that rivaled the roaring waves beside us. "You don't know how they reacted. You weren't there. A submarine ride won't fix this."

"Tell me what I can do. Let me talk to Casey. I heard her date went badly, and I know it was because of me. Maybe she was taking some of that out on you this morning," I tried to reassure her, but she was shaking her head, unable to meet my eyes. I knew some of Casey's anger was meant to be directed at me, but Jenna took the brunt of it in my absence, and it made me feel sick.

"We were selfish and we hurt her, Travis. Both of us." Jenna's voice was less animated now, a cold acceptance. I scooted closer to her, but she pulled away. "I needed you today. And you abandoned me for work, right after you promised me you'd never be like my mom."

Jenna sounded so hurt as she folded her legs up into her arms and cried. I felt terrible. I had abandoned her for my work, but it wasn't like I had just disappeared all day. I told her it was an emergency. Still, my entire body was aching as

I watched her, unable to come up with words that could fix this.

"I am so sorry. Jenna, look at me." I put my hands under her chin, wiping away the trail of tears on her soft skin. "Sometimes my work pulls my attention, but that doesn't change how I feel about you. You come first, and I know it didn't feel like that today. I—"

"I just think you've changed too much, Travis. Maybe we're chasing something that we should have left in high school, or that should have never even begun."

It felt like she had just ripped my heart out of my chest and threw it into the sea. I was drowning.

"That's not true, Jen. We're perfect for each other."

"How can you say that after what we just did to Casey?"

"Casey just needs time to sort out her feelings. She'll see how right we are and she'll be happy for us. I promise."

"Stop making promises you can't keep!"

"Jenna—"

"I want to go home." Her words were final. There was no swaying her tonight, I knew that. So, I acquiesced.

"I'll arrange for a plane to pick you up tomorrow." I stroked her cheek, trying to soak in as much of her as I could before she left.

"Thank you," Jenna said softly. She stood and wiped the sand off her legs, turning back towards the house without another word.

17

JENNA

I woke up feeling the heaviness of what we had done. My eyes were still puffy from my sobbing and my heart ached for my best friend.

Casey was one of the most important people in my life. I loved her and I didn't want to hurt her. I had seen the look in her eyes when she'd confronted us—she had felt betrayed and angry, so hurt, and the expression had put a lump in my throat that still hadn't gone away. I didn't know what I'd do if she couldn't forgive me.

My heart ached from Travis too. He abandoned me when I needed him most. I knew this deal was important to him, but it made me wonder how many more important deals or work emergencies would pull him away from me. He didn't seem to fully understand how much his absence hurt—not just because it left me alone to deal with Casey, but because it felt way too similar to the gaping hole my mom left behind every time an art show or an auction took precedence over me.

I packed my bags slowly, working up the courage to face everyone. Once I had finished, I put my hair in a ponytail, took a deep breath and walked downstairs. Only Alice stood in the kitchen. I looked around for any sign of Casey, but she was nowhere to be found.

"Good morning, dear," Alice greeted me with more warmth than I expected, or deserved.

"Um, morning," I said, pushing a stray lock of hair behind my ear. I knew I still looked disheveled from yesterday.

"Come, sit." Alice motioned for me to join her at the table.

"Okay." My voice cracked a bit as I held back tears.

"I'm so sorry, Alice. I know I betrayed you all."

.   .   .

"You didn't betray us, Jenna. I was just surprised. I think we both were." Alice looked at Casey's empty chair.

"Do you think she'll ever forgive me?"

"I think she'll come around." She reached over to rub my back in circular motions just as Travis had last night. A sob broke through. "Oh, Jenna." Alice leaned in for a hug and I let my emotions loose, crying into her shoulder.

"I think I lost him too," I said. Alice took a deep breath.

"In hindsight, I'm not sure why I was so surprised. As kids, you and Travis were always running around, flirting and teasing each other. It was quite cute," Alice told me with a little chuckle, trying to ease my nerves. "I have no doubt things will work out with time, and even if you and Travis don't end up together, know you'll always be a part of this family."

· · ·

"Thank you, Alice." I didn't know what else to say. I couldn't thank her enough for everything she had done for me. She just gave me a tight squeeze and helped me take my bags to the limo Travis had waiting. Casey never showed.

A driver took me to the hangar on the island where a private jet was waiting for me. I boarded the plane and sat back in the comfortable recliner with a sigh. A steward offered me champagne, but I refused. Shutting the window shades beside me, I pulled out my journal and began to write about everything; my conflicting feelings for Travis, my desperation to get my best friend back, my lingering pain from my mother. I wrote until my hand ached and my tears stopped, and then I slept.

I woke to the jet's wheels hitting the ground. Home. I was back home. My plan was to stay in Maplewood for the night and then head back to Yale first thing in the morning. I could get ahead in some coursework for the last few days of break and squeeze in some shifts at work. I wanted to pay Travis back for the trip, especially considering everything that had gone down.

I gathered my things and made my way off the plane, squinting as a ray of sun beamed off of my face, until my vision cleared enough for me to see giant white letters in the distance. HOLLYWOOD. In a panic, I scoured my surroundings, stopping at a familiar face.

18

TRAVIS

*J*enna deboarded the plane in a confused rage. I watched as she aggressively fumbled with her suitcase handle and stomped down the stairs. I would have laughed under different circumstances.

"What the hell am I doing here, Travis?"

"Realizing that we are meant to be together," I told her, stone cold and serious.

"Oh yeah? Because I'm pretty sure someone who I'm supposed to be with would have listened to me when I said I just wanted to go home! Especially after how that *someone* had just treated me."

"This can be home, Jen. Let me show you around LA, show you why I love my job here, and show you how easily and happily you'd fit in."

"Is this your version of an apology?"

"It's a start," I smirked.

"Don't smile. What about Casey? Spending the weekend with you is not going to go over well and I won't jeopardize our friendship any further." Jenna's arms were crossed and her brows furrowed. She was so cute, even when she was angry at me.

"I have something up my sleeve for Casey. Within a couple days, everything should be just fine." I gave her sly grin, not willing to reveal my plan just yet. I wanted Jenna to be just as surprised as Casey. "Please, let me prove to you that you come first. And let me show you why I've been so distracted."

This caught her attention. Jenna wanted to trust me, I knew she did. Just as much as I knew I had to work to earn back that trust. I was willing to climb mountains to make her understand my affections.

"Fine. But this time, as soon as I say I want to go home, even if it's in 5 minutes from now, you listen." She waved her finger at me and I nodded with a smile. I loaded her bags into my Mercedes, which got an eye roll from Jenna, and we took off.

We arrived in Los Angeles around dinner time, and I brought Jenna to my penthouse first thing so that we could rest and change before we went out to my favorite restaurant, a little Italian place that was nothing expensive or fancy but had the best food in the city and the most beautiful view of LA. I had reserved the entire restaurant for the evening, ensuring that we'd have privacy from any press that could ruin my deal and that we'd be able to enjoy each other's company with no distractions.

I watched her face as we reached the top of my building, the elevator opening directly into the penthouse. The place was massive, all one floor, with wide floor-to-ceiling windows that looked out onto the city. She stood there for a long moment, looking out, drinking in the view with awe on her face.

"It's beautiful," she breathed. It was getting dark outside, and the streetlights had just flickered on. The whole city looked like it was lit by fairy lights, bright white and sparkling hundreds of feet below. I couldn't look out the window, though. I was taking in a different view, looking at Jenna as my heart did a flip in my chest. She was the most beautiful thing I had ever seen, even prettier than the skyline of the city I loved.

"I want to get changed before dinner," she said, her voice still stern. I showed her to the master suite. "Do you mind?"

"Can I watch you?" I asked her. She gave me a shy smile, but it fell almost immediately. Before she could say no, I nodded and left, giving her some privacy. I was determined to do things right this time around, and right now, Jenna needed space to organize her thoughts about us.

After we were both changed, we walked to the restaurant, which was only a few blocks from my building. On the way there, I grabbed Jenna's hand, slowly at first to get her permission. Once I had it, I eagerly laced our fingers while we walked. Just being with her felt natural and perfect; holding her hand was enough to make me desire her all over again. At this point, my worries about being seen with her in public were fading. The deal would be over by tomorrow. Besides, as I scoured the passersby, no one seemed to care one bit about Jenna and I. I let the tension in my body relax, and made up my mind to enjoy this night with Jenna. No more work distractions,

By the time we got to the restaurant, I lingered outside wanting desperately to kiss her. I held her close and she let me. I leaned my head down and briefly tasted her mouth before we went inside. When I pulled away, she was smiling softly. I hoped she had missed our kisses as much as I did.

We were seated at a table outside in the quaint little garden where the restaurant grew their own vegetables.

There were flowers, too, blossoming in every corner. The restaurant was situated at the top of a hill, allowing it to overlook downtown. Jenna took in another gorgeous view, with satisfaction written all over her face. It was the same face she had made when I touched her in Florida. The realization made the blood rush to my face. She noticed the Hollywood sign in the distance and promptly rolled her eyes, no doubt remembering her grand entrance this morning. This made me laugh.

"So, you're going to show me your office?" she asked after we ordered our food and a bottle of wine to share.

"I thought I would," I said. "Tomorrow morning. I have a few things to take care of, actually, and I thought they might be of interest to you." My eyes were beaming as I spoke to her, laced in mystery. I could tell she was intrigued.

"Like what?" she asked and I was glad that she seemed eager. I didn't want to bore her on this trip—I wanted to show her all of the best parts of the place that I loved the most and called home, and I wanted to prove that she could trust me. This trip to my office would do just that.

"You'll just have to wait and see." I grabbed her hand and brought it to my lips, never breaking our gaze.

"Tonight," I continued, "I thought we'd stay in."

"Oh okay." I could see her cheeks reddening as she thought of all the things I might do to her this evening. I watched her contemplate, wondering if she'd let me. If Jenna wanted to take things slower, this time, then I'd do it in a heartbeat. We could watch a movie on the opposite side of the room if she wished. As long as she was with me, I was more than happy.

"Or we could walk the city if you'd rather. Anything you'd like." I grinned at her and she sheepishly smiled back, looking down at her plate of noodles that had just arrived.

"Staying in sounds nice," she said, taking a sip of her wine in a way that drove me wild. "What else are we going to look at while we're here?"

"It depends," I tried to catch my breath as I watched her. "Are you interested in touristy stuff?"

She seemed to think about it for a minute. "Not really."

"Good," I said, relieved at her response. "I'll take you on my private tour of the city tomorrow."

"Are there a lot of special places here?" she asked. "You haven't been here for very long. How do you know the city so well?"

"I went out a lot when I first moved here. Went for walks, explored the city. It's something that I like to do when I'm on my own to clear my head."

"Does it work?" she asked.

"Sometimes."

"And what is it you think about, Travis? What can't you get out of your head?"

"Work," I responded. "And now you. Maybe only you from now on."

She blushed, and the look was so sweet that it spread warmth and light throughout my body. We finished dinner and walked back to my place, both of us eager.

19

JENNA

This entire day had been a whirlwind of emotions. I was so pissed at Travis for flying me here, but I was also tempted by the chance to get to know his world better. Despite trying my hardest to push away any and every feeling I had for him, I still loved Travis. And his annoying, but romantic gesture showed me how much he loved me. It made me realize that maybe I could fit into his world and maybe he hadn't changed as much as I thought he had. Plus, he had a plan to get us back on Casey's good side.

Travis hovered across the room from me, his eyes only on me. I knew I could easily ask him to just watch a movie with me and he'd happily acquiesce, but that's not what I wanted. I felt the heat of his stare on me and it made my body tingle. My pussy swelled as I remembered his touch on our cove on the beach. I wanted to feel that again. I wanted to be close to him, to savor every touch.

"Can you come here?" I asked him, pulling down the shoulder of my sweater, showing him what I wanted. Travis stalked closer, a lion on the prowl. He let out a low growl as I pulled my top down further, revealing my lacey red bra.

Travis wrapped his hand around my hip and pulled me close, his cock pressed against my pussy through the fabric of our clothes. I found my body rubbing up against him, desperate for some relief from the tension that was building up inside of me. He responded by slipping his tongue into my mouth. I wanted him so bad that I tried to undress him, but he took my hands and held them still as he grinded against me instead. I felt like a teenager going to second base for the first time; even touching him like this outside of our clothes was a wonder to me in how good it felt. He took my mouth in another kiss, the length of his cock taunting me. I squirmed out of his gasp, taking my sweater fully off before he could stop me. I could tell by the look on his face that he hadn't wanted to stop me, anyway. My breasts were firm and heavy as he released the clasp on my bra and let it drop to the floor. He cupped them in his hands and stroked my nipples with his thumbs.

He pinched them between his thumbs and forefingers, tugging on them lightly while I wiggled out of my panties, kicking them off so that I was naked. Every time I tried to undress him, he stopped me. I wanted our skin pressed together and hated every bit of fabric between us.

"Travis," I whimpered, his cock grinding against my clit. "Please don't do this."

He groaned softly at my words, pulling back slightly to strip himself of his clothes and put on a condom. When he was naked, he pulled me against him again so that we were lying face to face on the bed, our bodies pressed together. I wrapped my leg over his hip, parting my legs for him so that he could slip his cock inside of me. The moment he filled me up, I sighed, feeling relief from the pressure that had been building inside of me. He held onto my leg, digging his fingers into my hips as he rode against me, sliding his cock in and out of my pussy in a tantalizingly slow way.

"You fit me so perfectly, Jenna," he said. "So tight and wet on my cock. Your pussy was made for me."

I kissed him in agreement, wrapping my leg around him tighter to pull him deeper. The way he was moving against my hips was making me feel out of control, my eyes rolling back as I took his cock over and over. He pulled out of me then, leaving me empty and bereft, and I pouted at him as he grinned and kissed my throat.

"Turn around," he said, twirling his finger so that I knew to flip over. I turned on my other side so that my back was to him, pressing my ass back against his cock and wiggling it against him. He growled and I gasped when he brought his hand down on my ass to spank it, sending a surprise sting of pain through my skin.

"You trying to tease me?" he asked. I wriggled against him again, reaching back between my legs to take his cock and pull it forward. I rubbed it against my pussy with my hand as he lifted my leg up, then guided it into my pussy from behind. The angle filled me with a new sensation, especially when I realized that his every thrust in this position hit me in such a sweet spot that it made me moan aloud, even though I was trying to be quiet. He reached around me and put his hand over my mouth as he rode against me.

"That's the spot, isn't it?" he asked. "Does that feel real good, baby?"

I nodded, my mouth still muffled by his hand. I was grinding back against him, taking him deep inside of me.

"Oh my god," I moaned as he started to rub my clit with his hand. The sensation of pleasure was too much and I tried to close my legs, but he was grasping me tight so that I was forced to keep them open. With him fucking me in all the right ways, hard but slow and deep, I forgot every worry in my head and could focus only on the pleasure in my body. "Oh my god."

"You can come," he said. "I'm not going to keep you from coming tonight. I want you to do it for me over and over."

"Thank you," I breathed as he sped his hips up. I turned my head to the side and he lifted his face to kiss me as I came for the first time, squirming against him. He kept going, rubbing along each side of my clit when it was too sensitive to touch it directly, teasing it with the tip of his finger once I was ready again. I came again, shuddering, crying out in his mouth. Still, he kept going, until I shattered with pleasure for a third time and was breathing heavily, my body slack and exhausted. He came a little while later just grinding inside of me, his fingers stroking the outer lips of my pussy. When we were finished, he pulled out of me and I cuddled back against him again, pulling his arm around my waist.

Travis kissed my neck. "Go to sleep, baby. Everything is going to be okay. Tomorrow, you'll see."

"Okay," I said. I hadn't mentioned Casey all night, but he knew my best friend still weighed heavily on my mind. I began to lower my guard against Travis today, wanting desperately to trust him again. I closed my eyes, and found myself dozing easier than I thought I would, anxious for tomorrow to come.

20

TRAVIS

Jenna and I spent the morning locked together, making as much noise as we wanted to now that we were alone. The sound of Jenna moaning was the sexiest thing I had ever heard, and the harder I fucked her the louder it got. I made up my mind to make her scream and spent the entire morning dedicated to it. We woke up at sunrise and didn't shower until almost noon.

After we had finally collected ourselves, both of us reeling from our activities, I led Jenna to the car, jittery and excited for the day ahead. My office was at the very top of a skyscraper, one of the tallest buildings in Los Angeles. I walked Jenna through the building, stopping on the first floor to show her the café and the architecture, which was regal and elegant.

Before we could make it upstairs, we were blinded by flashes and camera clicks. Jenna covered her eyes with an outstretched hand, squinting past the lights. I stood in front of her, trying to block her from the paparazzi, but they had surrounded us.

"Shit." My stomach dropped. I couldn't let any photos surface of Jenna and I, not today. I still needed to close this deal and a photo of me next to another woman in the press would surely spread like wildfire and might jeopardize everything. Plus, I could see how nervous Jenna was, her breathing accelerated and shaky. I needed to get her out of here.

Just then, my assistant Scarlet came running through the lobby, screaming at the press in a failed attempt to shoo them away.

"Take Jenna!" I yelled at Scarlet. Jenna looked at me, surprise flooding her face as I handed her off to my trusted assistant. I watched as she grabbed Jenna's hand and escorted her away.

When the cameras finally dissipated, I made my way up to my office, still seeing stars from the flashes. Shooting off a text to Scarlet, I entered the conference room to find Devinia, her father, and Arthur, with papers strewn across the table in front of them.

"Afternoon, everyone," I greeted them.

"Travis!" Devinia stood up and rounded the table, her arms outstretched for a hug.

"Hi Devinia. Good to see you." I tried to sound cordial.

"I've missed you, babe," she flirted as she gave me a peck on the cheek. I froze at her touch, trying to gain my composure.

"Are we ready to do this?" I attempted to redirect their attention back to the deal. I looked to Devinia's father, who was observing our exchange with a pen in his hand.

"I'm ready when you are," he replied.

Devinia pouted a bit, but sat back down, her thumbs running across her phone screen at rapid speed. I imagined she was posting her thirtieth photo of the day.

Arthur passed out the deal, so that a fresh copy sat in front of everyone. We proceeded to read through it in its entirety. I kept anxiously looking at the clock, knowing Jenna was probably bored out of her mind. I was hoping to have her sit in on the signing, but Scarlett texted me saying Jenna was still a little shaken. She told me she could take care of her, until I was done. As Arthur read the deal out loud, I thought of where I'd take Jenna for dinner, to reveal my big surprise.

"Alright, everything looks good on our end," Arthur announced.

Devinia's father stood up and shook my hand after he signed the last page.

"Pleasure doing business with you, son," he said.

"You as well, sir," I told him.

Devinia looked up from her phone. "Are we done here?"

"We are."

Devinia sulked over to me once again, and I almost felt bad for her. Yeah, she was a pretty awful girlfriend when we had dated, and she did use me. But, her life seemed pretty lonely and her career hadn't taken off quite like she had expected. On top of the publicity I provided her, I think she appreciated my company, even when we were no longer romantically involved. I was, however, looking forward to not having to put on a show with her in front of the cameras anymore.

"Well, it's been fun, but it's about time we broke this thing off, isn't it?" I tried to keep things light.

Devinia smiled, "It's been fun, baby. I really don't want it to end."

She gave me another kiss on the cheek and that's when I noticed Jenna in the doorway, her face showing a mix of shock and devastation.

21

JENNA

"Oh, I think they are finally done in there!" Scarlet exclaimed and I looked behind me to see feet shuffling from the lower window of the conference room. The rest of the shades had been shut, shrouding their meeting in secrecy. "You can go in now," she said, getting up from behind her desk.

Scarlet had talked my ear off for over an hour, trying to loosen my nerves after the paparazzi run in. She told me how amazing of a boss Travis was and how much she loved working under him. Scarlet told me about some of Travis' biggest deals, but said this one seemed particularly important to him. He was keeping it a surprise from most people. I tried to listen—Scarlet seemed very nice—but my thoughts were elsewhere.

• • •

I couldn't stop replaying the incident in my head: lights flashing, Travis shielding me from the cameras. Eventually, Travis pushing me off to Scarlet, like I was a lost, annoying puppy. He clearly didn't want to be seen with me in front of the cameras. I was a nobody and I guess being seen with me wasn't a good look. I was hurt and deflated. I walked next to Scarlet with my head down.

"It's about time we broke this thing off, isn't it?" I heard Travis say as Scarlet opened the door to the meeting room for me. I looked up and Devinia was leaning in for a kiss.

"It's been fun, baby. I really don't want it to end," she said to him in the most seductive tone I had ever heard. Her lips left a red mark on his jawline.

I gasped, both of them looking up from their exchange. At first, Travis looked surprised, then extremely worried. I had caught him in the midst of breaking up with Devinia.

"How dare you?" I exclaimed.

Devinia began to smile, her eyes filled with amusement. Travis just looked at me speechless.

.   .   .

"Was this your big plan? Quickly dump her behind my back so you wouldn't be caught in a lie? And then, what? Move right on to the next girl? Wow, I guess I should have believed those rumors about you," I said and I could tell that my words stung by the pained look on his face. He had told me not to read too much into his reputation, and I had believed him so easily.

"Jenna, it's not what you think. We were just signing off on this deal." Travis tried to hand me some papers but I swatted them away.

"I get why you were so embarrassed to be seen by the paparazzi with me now. It all makes sense." I thought back to the lingerie at the beach house and the photos on Devinia's Instagram. He had been lying all along.

Instead of responding to me, Travis looked to Devinia's dad.

"I paid them off," Travis told him. "The paparazzi deleted the pictures of us."

. . .

D evinia's dad nodded and I let out an incredulous laugh.

"W ow, I'm out of here," I said, putting my hands above my head in surrender as I walked out. I was so done with Travis' games.

"J enna, wait! Let me explain!" Travis tried to run after me, but he was stopped by a delighted Devinia.

"Let her go, Travie. You can do so much better." Those were the last words I heard before I left his office, tears streaming down my face. I ran back to Travis' apartment to pack my bags, hoping I could be gone by the time he returned.

O nce packed, I walked around Travis' penthouse restlessly as I waited for my Uber to arrive, pacing in a circle like a cat. I felt irritated and on edge. Travis had brought me to his job under the guise of showing me around but had disappeared on me, leaving me alone with his secretary—all to break up with Devinia without me knowing.

· · ·

I should have known, though. It made me uncomfortable to think about and I wondered again if I was just a trophy for him, his little sister's best friend, someone who was sexy because she was off-limits. He probably would have dumped me as soon as he got tired of the novelty of it all. I swallowed, feeling a heaviness in my chest just thinking about it. He was so convincing in Florida. The way he looked at me, touched me; it felt like love. He assured me over and over again that he and Devinia were done. He was such a good liar, I wasn't sure how I'd ever know what, if anything, was real.

I felt almost sick. I was falling for Travis, if I hadn't already fallen for him completely. I hurt my friend to be with him—ugh, Casey. This was such a colossal mess.

About twenty minutes passed and my car finally arrived. As I was leaving the building, Travis came running down the sidewalk. His hair was wind blown and his face was flushed, like he had run the entire way back. His face held an apologetic look as he ran his hand through his hair, but now it all felt like a show.

"I'm so sorry, Jen," he said, coming to me. He put his hands on my shoulders and I didn't pull away, couldn't pull away. The only thing I could do was stare at him. I wondered who he was and what he had become. The Travis I knew in high school didn't exist anymore, and the Travis who had taken his place wasn't somebody that I could be with. "What you saw wa—"

"Save it. I wouldn't believe a thing you said anyway." I pushed him off of me, cold and broken.

"Jen, it was a business deal. One that I couldn't pass up. The only reason I'm able to provide for my family is because I make these sacrifices. Just let me explain," he pleaded.

"Everything is a business deal to you, isn't it? You play with people's feelings as a means to get whatever you want. How many people have you shattered to get to where you are?"

I had a feeling I wasn't the first one who had been completely devastated by his lies. He was a playboy, and a cutthroat billionaire. Maybe he did believe the words he was telling me, but that didn't make any of it real. Before he could respond, I got into my Uber and slammed the door shut, locking it and telling the driver to take me to the airport.

22

JENNA

I managed to sleep on the plane ride, reacclimating myself to coach. I had been spoiled over the past week with the private jets. Instead of staying for a night in Maplewood like I had planned, I immediately got into my car and drove to Yale, anxious to put as much distance between myself and the pain as possible.

When I got back to school, I was still exhausted. I felt tired through every bone in my body, and just wanted to lay down in my bed forever. I kept thinking about Travis and wondering where it all went wrong, where the truth stopped and the lies began. I loved being with him and loved it when he touched me, but then I thought about my own dreams. I wanted more out of life than to constantly be neglected and lied to, stuck at home waiting for someone who would never really be present, not as long as he had work on his mind and a playboy status.

I thought about Casey again and pulled out my phone. I wanted to tell her that it was over with Travis, apologize, and tell her that I'd made a huge mistake. I only hoped that she would be willing to talk to me in the first place. Casey could be stubborn when she was angry and could hold one hell of a grudge. I had always known that about her, but I had never thought that I would be at risk of being on the receiving end of that anger. I threw my phone face down in front of me, too scared to make the call. Right now, I could pretend that we were going to be okay in time, but if I called and received a final rejection from Casey, I didn't know how I'd cope.

I kept myself busy with work until classes started back up. Once classes began, I barely had any time or energy to think about Travis or Casey. I blocked everything that hurt from my thoughts and just focused on me. I began to write often, during any small ounce of free time I had, out of fear that my thoughts would drift to Travis or that my guilt about Casey would overwhelm me. But I also started writing because it was a good outlet. During the time my pen was on paper, I felt slightly more whole, and more hopeful about the future, regardless of who may be in it.

After several weeks of writing and processing, working and studying, I finally worked up the courage to confront my best friend. I needed her. So, on a Friday after my classes, I hopped in my car and made the two hour drive back to Maplewood, nervously shaking the entire time. I blasted the radio all the way up, trying to drown out the thoughts in my head, thoughts of Travis and what might have been if things were different, thoughts of Casey and how this apology would go. The music didn't work. I'd just have to endure until I saw her. I knew I deserved to feel this guilt anyway. With each mile marker, I grew more anxious. If she didn't forgive me, I'm not sure any amount of writing or avoidance could heal that wound.

I pulled up to a recognizable porch, the flower arrangements still blooming in their pots. Before I could convince myself otherwise, I knocked on the door. I remembered back to several weeks ago, when Casey told me that I never needed to knock. Our friendship had changed a lot since then.

Alice opened the door, looking surprised to see me.

"Jenna! How are you, my dear?"

"I'm okay." I smiled at Alice. "I was hoping to talk to Casey, actually. Is she here?" I asked, peering into the house.

"Oh, no she isn't. She's at the coffee shop. I was just heading over there, though. I can take you, if you'd like?"

"Um, yeah sure. That would be great."

Alice sent off a few texts and then grabbed a small wrapped package before we headed out. I eyed it curiously, but she didn't say a thing. During the drive, I asked Alice if she had heard about LA. She had. Travis had come home not too long after I left and told her everything.

"I was sorry to hear it, Jenna. I'm so glad to see you. I think Casey really has missed you," Alice told me as we pulled into the cafe's parking lot.

I looked at the sign hanging off the front of the shop, and a jolt of amazement coursed through me. It no longer said The Maple Leaf in a dull red and brown. Now, the sign was sporting a fresh coat of aqua and sea green. The colors reminded me of Casey and I's snorkeling adventure; the beautiful blue tint of the ocean and the green hued sea turtle that we had followed for as long as we could until we tired ourselves out. The memory made me smile. My smile grew when I noticed the new name: Casey's Cafe.

I ran into the shop to greet her. Stopping when I saw her long brown hair and curvy frame.

23

JENNA

"Casey," I spoke softly, cautiously. Casey turned around, not looking as surprised as I had expected.

"Hi," she said, inching closer to me.

"This, this is amazing, Case. I am so happy for you." I motioned to the shop, the interior of which was painted the same sea green.

"Thank you," she said, smiling at the ground.

"I am so sorry, Casey. It was all such a massive, selfish mistake."

Casey finally looked up at me, her brown eyes warm and comforting. I had missed that stare.

"I was just taken by surprise. I felt left out more than once on the trip, and then when I realized why, I just," she trailed off.

"You had every right to be upset. I broke our pact. I broke your trust and I can't apologize enough."

"It was a stupid pact." Casey laughed a little. "I was an angry teenager when we made it. I just wanted you to be honest with me, that's all. And I'll admit, I was a little jealous. I felt like I was losing you."

"I'll never lie to you again," I said, holding up my pinky in a promise. "And you'll never lose me."

Casey gave me a big smile and wrapped her pinky around mine.

"A new pact," she said.

Alice came into the store and motioned that she was going to use the restroom. Casey ordered a coffee for her mom and we sat down at a table by the window.

"So," I continued, still a little nervous. "I'm sure you heard, but Travis and I are over."

"Yeah, I heard," Casey said. "I'm sorry."

"It just wouldn't have worked out," I said, twirling the straw in my iced latte.

"It's a shame. I know I was sort of a brat about it, but I could see how perfect you were for each other. You complement each other well," Case grabbed my fidgeting hand. I sighed.

"It's okay to still love him, you know," she said.

"I don't love him," I insisted, even though as I spoke the words I knew they weren't true. But I would deny it until I didn't feel anything for him anymore. I had to, otherwise it was going to make me crazy to have lost him.

Casey gave me a look. "I saw you two together, remember? And I know you both. You're in love with my brother."

"I'm not. He lied to me," I said. "Like in a huge way."

Casey squeezed my hand again.

"I want you to be happy," Casey said.

"Yeah, me too. Let's just forget about it and move on," I said, still scarred from Travis' lies and my lingering feelings for him.

"So," I tried to change the subject, "Tell me how all this

happened!" I was genuinely so happy for my best friend. I knew how important this coffee shop was to her; she had finally made her dreams come true.

"Well." Smiling, she pulled out a piece of thick, white paper. I was so glad to see that look on her face again, and for a moment I didn't feel the pain of losing Travis anymore. "This is the deed!"

Casey placed the official-looking document in front of me. It was titled "Investment Agreement" and underneath it read, "Travis Winn and Bruce Barker." I thought back to Devinia's Instagram. Her last name was Barker. Bruce must be her father. I read further, my eyes widening as I discovered the truth.

This paper laid out the rules of Travis' deal, the one he had been talking about during the trip. He was to keep on good terms with Devinia, be seen with her and only her in the press for a period of three months. Her dad was hoping that being associated with Travis' reputation would help Devinia find her big break, but their breakup threw a wrench in those plans. This contract was his solution. He'd fund Casey's Cafe, but only if Travis helped his daughter get noticed.

My mouth dropped. Travis hadn't been lying. He wasn't with Devinia anymore and there was a reason I couldn't be seen with him by the paparazzi: Casey's dream. I looked up to Casey, who was no longer seated across from me at the table. I scanned the shop, stopping at a tall, handsome figure who had just emerged from the kitchen.

24

TRAVIS

Jenna stood in front of me, wide eyed and beautiful as ever. I rubbed my shaking hands, trying to suppress the nerves. I felt humiliated by the way things had ended—it was my fault entirely for neglecting her, for insisting that my work was more important and for not just being up front with her right away. I did it all for Casey, but I could have been more honest with Jen. I knew that now.

I was terrible to Casey too, sneaking around with Jenna behind her back. All while knowing full well how the same actions had made my sister feel in high school. I came home a week ago, to revamp the coffee shop and surprise Casey. I told her how sorry I was and that I hoped this could make up for even just a small fraction of it. Casey enveloped me in a hug, ecstatic about her cafe and happy to make amends.

Now, I had to try to make amends with Jenna, the woman I loved more than anything. I had realized this in Florida, but her absence in LA made it all the more real. I didn't put her first, and I'd never make that mistake again.

"Hi, Jen," I said, still standing across the shop from her.

"Hi," she responded, shocked.

"Look," I cut right to the chase, "I am so sorry for everything. I need you Jen. You mean the world to me, and you deserved better."

"I feel like an idiot. It was all for Casey and I got so angry with you. I never let you explain yourself." Jenna threw her hands in the air.

"No," I closed the distance between us, "No, I should have been honest with you right from the start. I didn't want to jeopardize the contract, and I honestly wanted it to be a big surprise for everyone, but instead I jeopardized our relationship. I should have just told you everything as soon as I saw how it was affecting you."

I grabbed Jenna's hands in mine and she looked up at me, her big green eyes radiating affection. I ran my hand through her hair and rested it on her cheek.

"I forgive you," she told me. I wrapped her in a hug and lifted her off the ground. Jenna giggled, gripping me tightly.

"Thank you. I won't let you down again. I promise, and I'll keep it this time," I said with a smirk as I put her down.

"I trust you," Jenna said.

"I will do everything in my power to make you happy. I'll sell my company today i—"

"That's not what I want, Travis. I know how much your company means to you and I'd never want to take that away. I just didn't want to always feel like I was always coming in second to it," she told me and I knew she was thinking about her mom.

I rubbed her arms up and down, hoping to dispel her doubts. "You're first, baby. Always."

Jenna smiled and I continued, "I've loved you since the moment I met you."

Jenna laughed. "You were twelve."

"You were my first crush. My only crush. I never stopped thinking about you. I still can't get you off of my mind."

"Me too. And I love you too." Jenna's face turned a shade of red that I knew too well. It turned me on more than she knew.

"Good," I said, smiling at her. "Sweet girl."

"It's about damn time!" Casey exclaimed from behind the counter. "I'm so happy for you both. And for me! Jen, we've always been sisters, but now it'll be legal!"

Jenna looked at me, confused. I rolled my eyes, unsurprised by Casey's big mouth. "This is why I don't tell you things, Case!" I yelled as my sister covered her mouth with both hands, a smile still in her eyes.

"I guess that's my cue," my mom said as she came out from the backroom to hand me a wrapped box.

I unwrapped the package, kneeling in front of Jenna as the Tiffany blue box was revealed. She gasped, and I grabbed her hands. I looked into her eyes, filled only with love. I knew she'd be my forever and I wanted that to begin today.

"Jenna, will you marry me?"

25

JENNA

Travis knelt before me on one knee. I could see the affection in his eyes, and I felt it in his touch. My eyes filled with tears, and my cheeks hurt from smiling so large.

"Of course I'll marry you!" I exclaimed and Travis let out a sigh of relief, sliding the beautiful diamond ring onto my finger.

He rose to give me a hug. "I love you," he murmured into my neck, sending tingles down my spine.

I met his gaze and kissed him, pressing my mouth to his. Sparks exploded in my stomach as our lips met. He sucked tenderly on my bottom lip before deepening the kiss, tasting my mouth, wrapping his arms around my waist to pull my body against his. Lust and love both filled me at once, taking over my body, making me press against him as he kissed me. It had been way too long and I craved his touch, his warmth.

"Ahem," Casey cleared her throat. "Let the record show that I'm totally supportive of you two, but the whole PDA thing might take me some time," she joked.

Travis and I laughed. Alice gave me a hug. "You've always been a part of this family. Now it's official."

I smiled, hugging her back. I didn't think I could be any happier. Suddenly, the bell above the front door rang, signaling a customer's arrival.

"Sorry, we're closed for a private dinner," Casey said, not looking up from the cash register as she closed out the day's profits.

"Have room for one more?"

Casey's head snapped up, her focus now entirely on the man who had just walked in. It was Jack, from her date in Florida.

"What are you doing here?" Casey squinted at him.

Before Jack could speak, Travis jumped in. "I invited him. I feel somewhat responsible for how your first date went," he said. Jack chuckled a bit, most likely remembering it.

"Think we can try again?" Jack asked Casey, a gleam in his eye as he took her in.

"I make no promises about what I will and will not rant about," Casey said, standing a little taller than usual and blushing as she continued, "Or how long I do it for. But if you're okay with that, then um sure."

Jack laughed. "I would expect nothing less from you."

We all sat as Casey's chef brought out a beautiful five course meal. Smiles were glued to our faces. Casey and Jack played footsie the entire time, and Travis stroked my upper thigh in circles, driving me wild. Alice watched us all with a content look of happiness on her face.

Travis excused himself to wash his hands, looking at me with a familiar mischief in his eyes. He nodded his head towards the back hallway, motioning for me to follow just like he had in Florida. This time, I'd listen.

After a few long minutes, I excused myself, practically sprinting to him. I met him in front of the door to the back office, both of us eager. We went inside and turned the light on, locking the door behind us.

"Bad girl," he said. "You want me to fuck you in here, baby?"

"Please," I said, knowing he couldn't resist when I said that word. I had a feeling that he didn't want to resist, anyway. He wanted me as badly as I wanted him. I would always want him. I kissed him then, pulling him over to the desk that stood in the middle of the small space. I sat down on it and pulled him close to me, parting my legs so that he could stand between them. "Wait, is this Casey's office?" I hesitated for a moment.

"She'll never know," he said smiling. He leaned down to kiss my collar bone.

"Jenna," he said. "I have missed you so much."

"I missed you too," I whispered, not even knowing how much I meant it until I said the words aloud. I had been thinking about Travis ever since I left him, trying to suppress the thoughts as they overwhelmed me, especially when I was lying in bed alone at night. I couldn't help but to imagine what it would be like to have him beside me in my bed, touching and holding me each night. Now I knew that I would get to live that reality.

"Did you think about me while we were apart?" he asked.

"Yes," I said. "All the time."

He leaned in, kissing me, his hands on my hips as he pulled them against his.

"Did you think about my cock, Jenna? Did you miss it?"

"Yes," I repeated, grinding forward against him. He pulled back from me, reaching down to unbutton the jeans I was wearing. Even the feeling of his fingers brushing against my skin sent a shiver through me. I was filled with anticipation knowing that I would soon have him inside of me just like I'd been wanting since the last time he'd touched me. I had craved him ever since, and thought about it all the time.

He pulled my panties down and off with my jeans, then undressed himself so that he could pull his cock out. He started to pull my sweater off but I stopped him.

"Maybe we should just make this quick," I said to him. "In case they decide to come looking for us."

"Oh, absolutely not," he said, nipping my bottom lip with his teeth. "If you think for one minute that I'm not going to take my sweet time inside of your little pussy, you're wrong."

"Oh," I breathed as he kissed me, slipping my tongue into his mouth to tease his. He reached down with his hand to stroke my clit with the tip of his finger, rubbing it directly so that an all-consuming pleasure washed over me, forcing out a gasp. He knelt down then, pulling my legs apart so that he could see every bit of my pussy. I could feel that the tops of my thighs were wet already, and I started to squirm as he put his mouth there and started to lick them clean, not touching where I needed him most.

"You are the worst person I have ever met," I complained when he sucked on my clit for only an instant, just long enough to find a spot that made me gush with pleasure. He stood up again, slipping a condom from his pocket and putting it on before taking my mouth in a kiss. He teased my clit with the tip of his cock, pausing while I ached..

"Take it," he said against my lips. I obeyed his command and moved my hips forward, taking his cock as deep as it could go. I started to ride against him and he stood still, letting me use his cock how I wanted it. I found a spot that felt so good that I almost couldn't breathe, rocking against him with my legs wrapped around his hips.

"Fuck me, baby," I panted, wanting more from him. He was teasing me by making me do all the work and holding himself back.

"A little bossy now, aren't you?" He nibbled my neck, but refused to moved his hips, even as I bucked against his cock. "Such a bossy girl."

"Please," I said, about to explode with desire. "Fuck me hard.""

"A bossy girl who can beg," he slowly moved his cock inside me. "I like that." He looked me in the eyes for a moment and then raised an eyebrow. Then he thrust his cock in me,deeper and faster with each thrust. I wrapped my arms around his neck then as he started curving his hips, almost lifting my ass from the desk. I felt like I couldn't see, couldn't hear, couldn't do anything but feel as I closed my eyes and tilted my head back.. His cock felt so good inside of me, so perfect, and I dug my nails into his back while I moaned. I had forgotten for a moment that his family—our family—might hear me. I didn't care. I was so happy to be reunited with Travis that I forgot about everything else.

I whimpered as he began to pound into me, his hips riding against mine. We were shaking the desk, our bodies clapping together as every bit of passion we had been saving up built between us. Travis kissed my throat when I started to come, sinking his teeth into my neck as I bucked against him, crying out in pleasure.

"I could make you come over and over again," he said. "I never want to stop."

"Don't stop," I said, my mouth against his, and he didn't, but continued to fuck me until I came again on his cock. He came shortly afterward, pounding against my hips until he was finished.

He pulled out of me and wrapped his arms around my body, pulling me against his chest as he caught his breath. When I pulled back, he smiled at me, tracing my lips with his fingers.

"I love you, Jenna," he said softly, kissing me.

"I love you," I said. The look in his eyes was making my heart pound in my chest—it was so real, the love genuine and bright. He was holding nothing back from me.

"You are the best thing that's ever happened to me," he said.

I looked down at the sparkling diamond on my left hand; it was hypnotizing. Then, I looked back up at Travis to see that he was gazing at me with the softest, sweetest expression. It was somehow infinitely more captivating than the diamond. I kissed him, basking in the feeling of his arms around me, like I was finally where I belonged.

THE END

A GIFT FROM LEXI AURORA

Get your free book at freebook.lexiaurora.com

DID YOU LIKE *The Billionaire's Forbidden Kiss?*

Then you'll love Keeping Secrets from the Billionaire - Lexi Aurora's best-selling book.

After my new billionaire boss kisses me on the first day, I have two secrets to keep.

One is how hard it is to resist him.

And the second is the secret that could destroy his empire.

I've tasted ritz and glamour, and it did nothing but bite me in the ass.

So now I've got to provide for my son, my everything, and I'm willing to put up with this dead-end job and arrogant boss to do it.

But soon the boss is dominating my thoughts...and me. His kisses are addictive and his fingers know exactly where to touch me.

Maybe I could indulge once or twice.

I just need to remember he can never know the real me...or we'll both go down in flames.

How hard can that be?

Read Keeping Secrets from the Billionaire today.

PREVIEW: KEEPING SECRETS FROM THE BILLIONAIRE

1

CHAPTER ONE- JULIE

The red neon light for the motel was going bad. It buzzed and blinked all night long, turning my dingy two-bedroom room into a disco party. Tyler had danced himself into exhaustion, but then, that kid could sleep through anything. It was a blessing that he'd been a quiet baby, or I probably would have fallen apart. While I couldn't even begin to imagine my life without him, the circumstances of his birth hadn't exactly been the highlight of my life.

When morning came, I dragged my exhausted, sweaty self out of bed and into the shower. The water was as cold as the air was hot, but even the lack of hot water and air conditioning wasn't enough for me to try to find somewhere else to live. With my budget, the fact that the place was relatively bug-free and came with a mini-kitchen was more than I could ask for.

"Baby, are you up?" I called out as I brushed my wet, strawberry-blonde hair into a ponytail. With a four-year-old son to chase after and very little money, I didn't bother with make-up. It'd simply melt off anyway. I'd made my way to

California thinking I could raise my son in warm and sunny climates, but Las Pameros was mostly desert, and the sun baked everything in its path.

"Momma, did you get some blueberry Pop-Tarts? I think I'd like some blueberry Pop-Tarts." My ever-so polite son rubbed his eyes as he walked into the bathroom and stared at me. With his blue eyes and blond hair, he was almost the spitting image of his father.

Pretending to think it over, I narrowed my eyes and studied him. "If I remember correctly, I told you yesterday that I would only get some blueberry Pop-Tarts if you could recite the information that I gave you."

"My name is Tyler Garner Dennings. My mother's name is Juliette Christie Dennings. I am four years old." He went on to correctly announce his address and the new phone number that I'd given him to memorize since I'd lost my phone three days ago and had to get a new one. My stomach twisted as he correctly recited the number for the local police and went over the stranger danger rules. In a year, he would be five, and I'd have a decision to make. It wasn't fair to keep moving him around when he started school, but it was also dangerous to stay in one place as well.

My kid was smart, and I wasn't just being a biased mother. He picked up things quickly, and he absorbed everything around him. It was almost a little terrifying.

Stumbling over a few of the numbers, he righted himself and looked at me with hopeful eyes. "Well," I declared loudly. "I think that might get you two blueberry Pop-Tarts!"

"Two!" His eyes shined with excitement, and I nodded my head as he skipped from my bathroom into the kitchen. It was a good thing that he was already ready because I was running late.

Pulling on a pair of jean shorts and a button-up plaid

top, I slipped my sunglasses on my face and grabbed my things. My only friend and pretty much savior, Crystal, lived two doors down. Crystal didn't have any kids, but she worked out of her motel room and was more than happy to keep an eye on Tyler for me while I was at work. There was some sort of unspoken rule around here about not asking people why they'd ended up at the Sunny Side Up Motel, so I never asked Crystal her story, and she never asked me mine, but I'd felt obliged to give her some details. She did look after my son, and there was always the slightest chance that his father might turn up.

Crystal was about my age, twenty-seven, with the perfect body and a gorgeous face. I couldn't help but sigh with a little jealousy when she opened the door and her perfect rack bounced ever so slightly when she bent to give Tyler a hug. While I had those childbearing hips and an ass that I still claimed carried some baby-weight, my tits were pretty small.

Not like there was a damn thing I could do about it.

"Are you giving me half of your blueberry tart?" Crystal gasped as she accepted the gift. "Well, that's so sweet. You must know that I have something special planned for lunch."

"What's that?' Tyler asked while I whipped out my phone and connected with Crystal's Wi-Fi. The motel internet was a joke, and Crystal had her own separate connection that she let me use.

"If I tell you, it won't be a surprise!" Crystal looked up expectantly. "Long day ahead of you?"

I knew that she thought my job was weird, and the truth was that I knew it was a little strange myself. I needed a cash-under-the-table kind of job, and I found it when I'd answered an ad for someone to run errands. By errands, my boss basically wanted to pay me a sliver of what she made to do her job. Darleen Mason was the personal assistant for the sinfully wealthy and handsome Graham Porter, but it was obvious that Darleen wasn't as interested in the work as she was the man. So while Mr. Porter paid her to keep his personal life organized, I was the one actually doing the work.

The truth was that it was a helluva lot better than some of the other jobs I'd done in the past, and Darleen never missed a payment.

"It looks like Darleen's boss has a birthday coming up." I'd signed a non-disclosure agreement, so I wasn't allowed to say who I was working for, but Crystal knew that it was some bigwig. "I have to pick up a present for him."

Crystal pursed her lips in disapproval. "I keep telling you, Julie. Something doesn't smell right about this job. How do you know you're not working for some mobster or drug kingpin?"

"You should be a writer," I laughed. "I'm fairly certain that isn't the case because things like that don't happen to me. Tyler, baby, I've got to run. Come give me some sugar." As always, when I left him, my emotions ran a little high, and my old Texas twang showed its ugly head. I'd worked hard to keep that accent down, but it popped up far more often than I would have liked.

My perfect son ran into my arms and gave me a big kiss on my cheek. I held him tight and inhaled deeply into his hair. He was the reason that I still breathed, and the reason that I was even doing all of this.

"Crystal says she's got something special for lunch," he whispered in my ear. "Last time she did that, we got McDonalds!"

God help me when things like McDonalds thrilled my

son. I let him go and paid Crystal for the day. The damn sign for the motel was still buzzing and blinking as I started my piece-of-crap car and drove to the boutique shops on Quarter and Main.

When I first started working for her, Darleen had given me a credit card to authorize expenses. I worried that someone would ask to see some identification, but it would seem that all the employers on the strip knew Darleen by heart and were told that I wielded her card. I hated using it. While Darleen had given me a job and paid me on a regular basis, that woman had a mean streak a mile wide. She threatened hell on earth if I ever used the card for personal reasons or if I ever told her boss what was really happening. When we did meet, the woman did nothing by criticize me up and down, but I tried not to mind. After all, I wasn't doing this for me.

I was doing it for Tyler.

Stepping into Matheson and Sons, the curio shop, my eyes immediately landed on a gorgeous wooden model ship that was encased in glass. The raw beauty of the ship spoke of someone's love and expert craftsmanship. It was unique, and it'd make a perfect ship for Mr. Porter. Generations ago, his family had made billions off the shipping industry, and while they had their hands in different pies now, I knew from my research that Graham Porter had a thing for ships.

"My nephew carved that," a gravelly voice said with pride. "His father would rather him be a lawyer, but it's rare to see that kind of talent these days. If you're interested, we can personalize the ship with a name of your choice."

"Your nephew has a gift," I said with a small smile. There was a time when I loved to be out on the water in a sailboat or kayak, but those days were long gone. "I'm actually here to pick up something that you're holding for Darleen Mason?"

The hope vanished from the man's face, and I immediately felt bad. The ship was out of place in a shop like this, and I gathered the man was having a hard time selling it. Moving slowly, the owner rounded the desk and reached under to pull out a box. When I opened it an peered inside, I immediately grimaced.

Nestled inside was the most god-awful looking statue I had ever seen. It was two lovers wrapped around each other and dipped in gold paint. If she gave that to Graham Porter, she might lose her job, and then I'd lose mine.

At least, that's what I tried to tell myself when I made the order to have Porter Shipping personalized on the carved model ship and returned the statue. The truth was that Darleen would never know until it was too late, and then she'd never admit that the ship wasn't her idea when she saw how happy it made her boss.

Maybe she'd even give me a raise.

I finished the errands and rearranging Mr. Porter's schedule, and the gift was ready just before the store closed. I paid for the gift-wrap and headed home. Maybe tonight, the damn sign would be out completely, and I'd be able to get some sleep.

2

———

CHAPTER TWO- GRAHAM

I stared in frustration at the computer in front of me and tried not to smash it to bits. There were a million things on my to-do list, and I couldn't remember the first one of them because my personal assistant had called in sick and failed to email me my schedule like she normally did.

Miles, my cousin, lounged in the chair across from my desk and kicked up his feet. We looked similar enough with dark hair and green eyes that he could have been my brother, but as far as personality went, we were night and day. I was reminded of that as I eyed his polished sized-thirteen shoe on my clean desk. "Don't you have something else to do other than bug me?" I snapped. "I thought you were leaving for New York today."

He chuckled. "Who knew that the great Graham Porter would be defeated by a computer calendar? Why don't you just call the damn woman and ask her to email it to you? Surely a cold wouldn't keep her from that."

"I tried," I muttered darkly. "I'm fairly certain that she's getting lipo or more Botox done. She was pretty much yelling at herself while she stared in the mirror yesterday."

My cousin shuddered. "Is there anything natural about that woman?"

Everything about Darleen Mason, from her permed, bottle-blonde hair to her bejeweled toenails were fake. I still wasn't sure why the hell she worked for me because I wasn't paying her nearly enough for those Double-Ds or the calf implants that she'd gotten to make her legs look shapelier. "Her eyelashes fell off the other day," I grunted. "Why the hell do women wear fake eyelashes?"

"She's hoping a few more surgeries might finally make her pretty enough to land you as a husband," Miles barked with laughter. "If only she knew how much you hated gold-diggers."

It was part of the reason that I would never settle down. Women were fun, hell, women were a necessity, but they were only good for a night or two before they started dreaming about glittering diamonds and shiny new cars, and hell would freeze over before I trusted a woman enough to deck her out in jewels.

"I've got it," I said with relief when I finally found the link to the calendar. I was about to click it when a notification for an email popped up on her computer.

Calendar Changes and Birthday Present.

"Fuck," I hissed. "I think Darleen is getting me a birthday present."

Miles' feet hit the ground, and he sat up in the chair. "Is it naked pictures? I'm dying to see if those things look as fake as they feel."

Lifting an eyebrow, I stared at my cousin. "And when exactly did you feel up my personal assistant?"

"When she *accidentally* fell into my lap the other day," Miles said with a frown. "I almost let her fall to avoid touching her, but I guess I'm not as big of an asshole as I'd like to be."

"Good. Maybe she'll start planning on marrying you instead of me," I said absently as I opened the email. It was addressed to Darleen from some woman named Julie, and it just confirmed that my present had been retrieved, and she'd made the changes to the calendar. *Suddenly sick my ass.* Darleen had clearly been making arrangements to have the next few days off.

When I closed the email, I realized that there was a long thread of messages between them.

Six-months long.

Scrolling through, I felt a wave of fury. "You've got to be fucking kidding me. That stupid, lazy bitch."

"Whoa. What the hell is wrong with you?"

"Darleen has been paying someone to do her fucking work for six months. For six months, someone named Julie has been given private information about my life." My eyes widened. "My God, Darleen gave her the notes from the investors meeting to type up."

"You thinking its someone working on the other side or someone from the press?" Miles asked tightly. A plane accident from five years ago left Miles and me as the only two remaining Porters left, and he had as much interest in our money as I did.

"I don't know, but I'm about to find out." Tension built in my shoulders as I composed an email from Darleen to Julie requesting that she meet me at the house so we could discuss some private details about what I wanted her to do next.

When she emailed me back and said that she wasn't comfortable meeting me at the house, I knew that I had her. "She must be someone that we know. I'm going to kill Darleen. I'm going to sue her for breach of contract, and then I'm going to make sure that no one who makes over twenty-thousand a year will want to fuck her."

I shot off another email insisting that I had private financial papers that needed drafting, and I couldn't have her do it in public. She emailed me back almost immediately agreeing.

The trap was set, and I was eager to see who I was about to catch.

"I guess I'm going to need another assistant," I growled as I slammed the laptop closed. The fake rhinestones glued to the top sparkled in the sunlight, and I had an urge to throw it out the window.

"Maybe make sure this one isn't going to pay someone else to do the job for them," Miles laughed.

"You think this is funny?" I demanded. "We've got millions tied up in this online banking company. If this Julie person really is a corporate spy, we could lose all that money."

"That would suck," Miles agreed. "But it's just a few million. I think we'll still get by. Have you made a decision about tonight?"

"You mean am I going to go out with you so you can have a shot with the triplets?" I asked as I stood and stretched. I was about to turn him down; the truth was that it had been too long since I'd had someone in my bed, their lips locked around my cock. This whole situation with Darleen had me desperate to blow off some steam.

Still, there was work that needed to be done. Regretfully,

I shook my head. I needed to make sure my head was clear when I met this Julie person tomorrow, and I didn't need another woman in my bed aiming for holy matrimony.

Keep reading Keeping Secrets from the Billionaire

ALSO BY LEXI AURORA

The Stonecutter Billionaire Series

Bound by the Billionaire

Bought out by the Billionaire

The Big Billionaire

The Forbidden Billionaire

Keeping Secrets from the Billionaire

The Billionaire's Nanny

The Stonecutters Billionaires Complete Series

Wrong: The Enemies-to-Lovers Series

Wrong for Me

<u>Wrong Kiss</u>

<u>Wrong Man</u>

Wrong Job

Wrong: The Complete Series

Real: The Fake Boyfriend Series

The Real Thing

The Real Deal

The Real Heat

The Real McCoy

Second: The Second Chance Romance Series

On Second Thought

A Second Look

A Second Shot

Shifters of Crystal Lake Forest

The Complete Series